TRAMP STEAMERS

MEME BLACK

TRAMP STEAMERS

A Budget Guide to Ocean Travel

Addison-Wesley Publishing Company

Reading, Massachusetts · Menlo Park, California · London

Amsterdam · Don Mills, Ontario · Sydney

Library of Congress Cataloging in Publication Data

Black, Meme.
  Tramp steamers.

  1. Ocean travel. I. Title.
G540.B37   910.4'5   81-37
ISBN 0-201-03776-9

Interior design by Susan Marsh
Cover design by David Rollert

ISBN 0-201-03776-9
ABCDEFGHIJ-DO-8987654321

First Printing, May 1981

To Joshua and Jonathan, and in memory of our pal Fergus

Contents

TRAMP STEAMERS

A Delta Line freighter off the west coast of South America
Delta Steamship Lines

ONE

SOUNDINGS

There's something incomparably thrilling about plowing through the vasty deep aboard a seafaring vessel. It's the ultimate in adventure—has been since the days of Odysseus. And whereas sea travel was once the exclusive province of the rich, cruising the high seas aboard opulent luxury liners, today freighters, those workhorses of the sea, make it possible for more and more travelers to experience the splendid pleasure of rolling seas and foreign ports.

So the word is out. Freighters take a few lucky passengers along on their voyages, often in surprisingly swanky accommodations. And what better time than now, when popular taste in vacationing has changed. Hard-working folks treasure their free time and spend months searching for just the trip to satisfy their wanderlust at the best possible price. Which is where freighters—called tramp steamers in deference to the term used in the thirties, the heyday of ocean travel—come in. These vessels traverse the seas, bound for exotic ports where few conventional cruise ships or even air tours go, at prices that boggle the mind and comfort the pocketbook.

You may still wonder exactly what a freighter is. There are several types, from those vessels principally engaged in toting cargo and licensed to carry a maximum of twelve passengers to the so-called cruise liners, which can take on more than twelve passengers and tend to offer somewhat more elaborate facilities—greater deck space, more stewards, wider choice of staterooms, swimming pool, and a medical doctor.

But whether freighter or cruise liner, here's a little-known fact about this means of conveyance. As freighters are laden with cargo and built with a wider beam, they glide more effortlessly across the waves than do their snootier relatives, the luxury liners. With most of the ship's weight riding well below the waterline, a freighter is less apt to roll or pitch in winds or high seas.

The dining room of a typical freighter, where passengers and officers often dine together

A freighter of the American President Lines laden with cargo passes beneath the Golden Gate Bridge, San Francisco. *South Street Seaport Museum Library*

Tramp steamers can take you virtually anywhere in the world, from Sri Lanka to Melbourne, Rotterdam to Mombasa, embarking from a number of East Coast, West Coast, Canadian, or Gulf ports. You also have the option of hooking up with a ship's itinerary in a variety of ways. For instance, you can sign on for a cruise—any round-trip voyage is considered a cruise by most freighter lines—and put in at each of your ship's many ports of call. Another option is to travel to one port, such as Rio de Janeiro, jump ship to explore the surrounding area for as long as you like then rejoin the cruise at another port along its itinerary.

There's yet another option: Most freighter lines accept one-way passage. You can fly to the Far East, for example, then make your way home by freighter, stopping at ports such as Manila, Bangkok, and Jakarta on the way, or leave from the United States by freighter and fly home from one of your ports of call.

At this point you may be thinking . . . sure, the travel promises excitement, but aren't those ships really rather *spartan?* Later in this book we'll provide personal testaments from enthusiastic tramp steamer travelers, but meantime suffice it to say that the accommodations on freighters are often comparable to those on luxury liners. The staterooms are large, liberally furnished, decorated by interior designers, air-conditioned, fully carpeted, and have large windows. With rare exceptions, staterooms are located on the outside of the ship (meaning with a porthole) and amidship, where the noise of engines and propellers can't be heard. (As you read about the ships in the guide that follows, be aware that there is a wide variety of rooms, particularly on cruise liners, ranging from a double room with a roll-out bed or upper berth to a deluxe stateroom with adjoining parlor.

The other facilities? Depending on the size of the ship, the freighter may have up to four or five passenger lounges equipped with television, stereo, games, bar, and snack pantry. Other services include: laundry room, barber and beauty shops, and a ship's store selling liquor, drug and cosmetic items, cigarettes, candy, and assorted sundries.

What about the dining rooms? What about the *food*? Cheerful, modern, and homey dining rooms—or saloons, as they are frequently called aboard—are situated on the highest deck to afford maximum light and view. As for the meals, food on freighters is notoriously delicious, with fresh baked-goods, succulent meats, and menus ranging from the national cuisine of the freighter line to familiar fare like pot roast. Hellenic Lines, for instance, boasts savory Greek dishes and wines. In general, freighter food tends to be far superior to that on luxury liners simply because freighter chefs cook for a small group, usually to order.

And what might you do to wile away the hours on a freighter? Well, after dinner you can wander out on deck with a woolly lap robe and a deck chair to watch the stars while the steward serves coffee or tea. By day, you can sun yourself, watch for schools of porpoises, and chat with newfound friends. Most freighters also have glassed-in observation decks for foggy or windy weather. And quite a few have swimming pools.

Finally, consider one of freighter travel's greatest treats—dining with the ship's officers (captain, first and second mates, chief engineer, purser), a garrulous, avuncular breed who delight in regaling passengers with facts and fancy about the sea, your ship, and your voyage's ports of call, not to mention tales of their own meanderings!

And speaking of the captain, here's another plus. On luxury liners only a map tells you where you're headed. On a freighter you're in constant contact with the officers, who gladly keep you posted on your route and the progress of the voyage, so you feel like a participant in the trip rather than merely a passenger.

In addition, inveterate travelers who have shipped out on both luxury liners and freighters swear that freighter passengers are treated like royalty. What's more, since all passengers are "in the same boat"—the highly graded class structure of luxury liners doesn't exist on freighters—everyone is similarly pampered by the crew, eats in the same dining room, and takes the air on the same decks.

In short, you get good treatment, repose, comfort, diversion, conviviality, and excitement without flattening your wallet. What is lacking are crystal chandeliers, orchestras, formal attire for dinner, and the like. Do

A stateroom aboard Delta Lines's "Explorer" cruise along the west coast of South America
Delta Steamship Lines

Spacious lounge on the *Enna G* of the Naura Pacific Line stretches the full width of the promenade deck, circled entirely by view windows. Port side opens to promenade, library, bar, sports deck, and swimming pool. Starboard side opens to dining room. *Naura Pacific Line*

Tramp steamers are hardly old rust buckets, as evidenced by this swimming pool on a Delta Lines ship. *Delta Steamship Lines*

you care? If you do, then freighter travel probably isn't for you. If you don't, then get ready to come aboard. But be warned—those who set out on one freighter trip tend to become habitual seafarers.

Among the many reasons Jesse and Clara Wallach of New York City choose to travel by freighter as often as they can are the congenial, sophisticated passengers with whom they share the ship. "Whenever we take a trip," says Jesse, "we're traveling with people like us. We swap travel stories, of course, but nobody comes aboard anxious to socialize. If you want to read in the lounge or write a letter, they respect your privacy. Freighter buffs are like that, really involved in the solitude and peace of an ocean trip." Clara agrees. "Everyone comes equipped with a pair of binoculars to look at sunsets and watch for passing ships. They—we—know what we want."

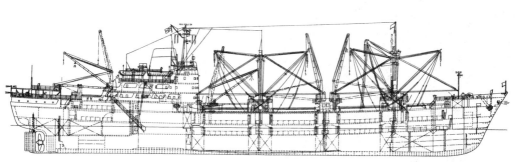

This cross section of a modern cargo ship shows the five cargo holds, including one divided into several rooms for chilled cargo. This 8,200 ton ship is of the shelter-deck type with fo'c'sle, bridge, and poop. *T. Tryckare*

Now just in case you're not ready to decamp immediately, ponder this: A typical luxury liner, the *Pacific Princess*, for instance, travels from Los Angeles to Honolulu via Christmas Island, Pago Pago, Sydney, and back in fifty-five days at a cost of $7590 (each) for a double stateroom. Lykes of the Lykes Lines makes the trip from San Francisco to Yokohama via Honolulu in thirty-two days for a mere $2050. (You'll find details of the Lykes trip in chapter 3.)

But before you start madly selecting an itinerary, here are a few important considerations to keep in mind. Freighters and cruise liners carry relatively small groups of passengers, and because this mode of travel is becoming more popular all the time, it's absolutely crucial to make your plans as soon in advance of your departure date as possible. For some trips, a year or more is not too early! (Not all demand such advance planning, of course.) The moment you've narrowed down your choices to a few trips, start the wheels turning. If you have ample time, write or call the freighter line directly. They will promptly send along brochures, rate sheets, and schedules. But if time is of the essence, and even if it's not, using a travel agent is probably the best way to proceed, since they know passenger booking agents at all the lines personally, can clue you in to some of the trickier aspects of planning a freighter trip, and may even be able to wheedle you onto an already booked trip. Passenger booking agents at freighter companies are very busy folk who can't always take time out to dispense advice, whereas travel agents have only one concern—you! Some agents who specialize in freighter travel are listed at the end of this book. Each is an expert highly recommended by freighter buffs.

When you do make your reservations, whether through an agent or the line itself, be prepared to pay a refundable deposit of from 20 percent to 30 percent, usually due within two weeks of booking. Final payment is

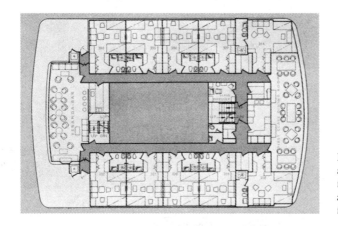

Floor plan of the accommodations for first class passengers aboard a typical freighter

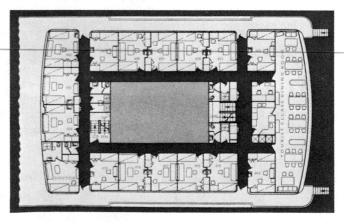

Tourist class accommodations

Cutaway view of S.S. *American Racer*—one of United States Lines' four newly reconstructed Containerliners in the company's New York-Antwerp-Rotterdam service   *South Street Seaport Museum Library*

then paid anywhere from one to three months in advance of your sailing date. (Cancellation within one month of sailing may cost a percentage of the total ticket.)

It's essential to remember one immutable fact as you plan your first voyage: the major function of freighters is transporting cargo. Schedules and ports of call are solely determined by the shipping needs of the companies whose products they tote. Thus ports of call may change at any time. This affects the cities you visit, the amount of time you spend in port, and the duration of your voyage. A travel agent can fill you in on guidelines and optional ports of call—as can individual freighter line's passenger agent—but be prepared to adapt to unpredictable schedules at times. Freighter buffs tell us they relish the spontaneity and excitement that comes with last-minute changes—and the awareness that visits ashore may at times be limited to a day, while on other occasions there will be a happy week to ramble around the port of call.

Be assured that your freighter line's representative and your agent will do everything possible to see that you're never inconvenienced. Also remember that at each port you're welcome to use the boat as your hotel. The ship's purser helps to arrange shore tours and sight-seeing.

One final fact, which we'll discuss in more detail in the trip descriptions: sometimes you return to a port that is different from the one your ship departed from. Just one more facet of freighter fun and charm.

Deck life aboard a steamship
W. T. Smedley

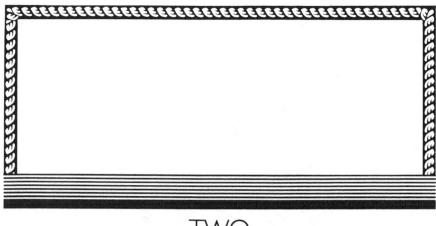

TWO

TIPS FOR A SHIPSHAPE TRIP

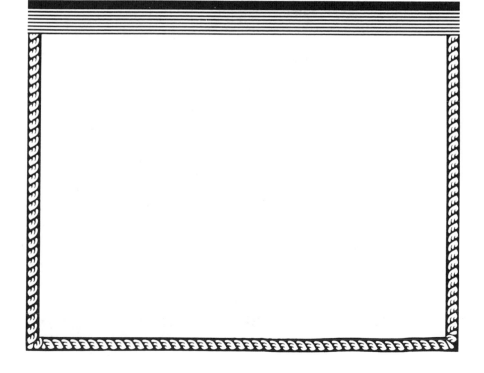

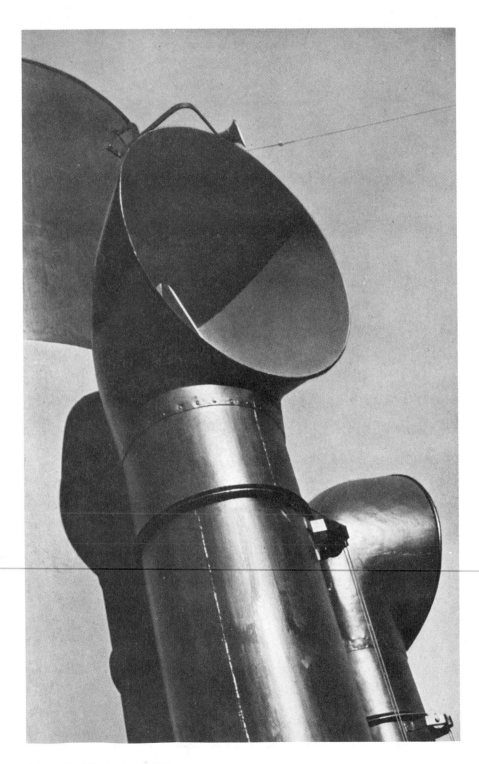

Some freighter lines vary their rates according to season. Hellenic Lines, for instance, charges slightly more during its "on season," May 1 to August 31, than during its "off season," September 1 to April 30. When this is the case, you will find both rates clearly noted on the table that accompanies each trip entry.

Freighter lines often impose age restrictions on older adults and young children. Ships that carry only twelve passengers have no doctor aboard, which is one reason for the rule. Conversely, cruise liners with resident physicians are usually more lax. Prospective passengers over the age of sixty-five may simply be asked to provide a certificate of good health attesting to their ability to make a long sea voyage. One can't generalize, however, since some lines don't accept pregnant women or children under the age of one year. Be sure to check with your travel or booking agent should any of these possible restrictions apply to you or a member of your traveling party.

As with any other travel outside the United States, you must have a valid passport or travel documents. Precise information regarding passport regulations is available from the Passport Office, Department of State, Washington, D.C. 20524, or from your travel agent. (Remember: minors over thirteen years of age need passports of their own.) Be sure your passport was issued within the past five years; if not, you must obtain a renewal. Getting a renewal passport takes about three weeks and can be done through either your local post office or divisions of the U.S. Passport Agency in major cities.

In addition to a passport, travelers who are not U.S. citizens must obtain an Income Tax Clearance Certificate (Sailing Permit) before sailing from the United States. Application must be made in person no more than one week before sailing at any office of the Internal Revenue Service.

Visas are, on the whole, not required to enter most European countries if you plan to stay for less than four months, although elsewhere they are an absolute requirement. Check with either the consulates or the embassies of the countries you plan to visit. Another possibility is to consult your travel agent; however, a travel visa specialist, such as Hazel Homes in New York, can obtain the required visas for you if you wish. Contact her at the Foreign Visa Service, 475 Fifth Avenue, New York, New York, telephone (212) 686-0934.

Another matter to check into well in advance is vaccination requirements. Some countries require a smallpox vaccination certificate proving that you've been vaccinated within the last three years. An International Certificate of Vaccination must be issued by the U.S. Department of Health, certified by a physician as well as an official of the board of health in the town where you reside. Also, certificates for cholera, yellow fever,

Ventilation funnels   *K. Helmer-Petersen*

The order is given to cast off. *International Nickel Co. Inc.*

typhus, and tetanus may be required by some countries. Ask your travel or booking agent about this matter—and for safety's sake, double-check with the U.S. Department of Health. Don't let a foul-up in paperwork ruin or delay your trip.

All Aboard

Anyone who has traveled farther than his or her backyard expects the issue of tipping to raise its ambiguous head sooner or later, and freighters are no exception. It's probably safe to say that on most freighters you need only tip the cabin steward, your dining room waiter, and perhaps any other steward who performs special niceties like bringing you an extra glass of orange juice in your cabin. Consult your travel agent as to the amount and any special customs of the line with which you travel. If you don't have an agent, you can simply ask the ship's purser, chief steward, or first mate. Generally, on brief trips you save all tipping until the end, while on a lengthy voyage you tip on a weekly or even biweekly basis.

We've said that freighter travel is an easygoing, casual affair. Thus when you pack for your trip, there's no need to contrive an elaborate wardrobe. Those who do only seem silly. As one witty freighter line manager told us: "Sometimes they come aboard with evening gowns and cigarette holders. What can they think—it's the QEII?" On the next page are some realistic considerations:

1 Remember you'll be aboard a ship. High heels won't do. Pack sneakers or other low-heeled, nonslippery shoes.

2 Even if you're traveling in the summer or to the tropics, bring suitable wraps, sweaters, or coats. Most freighter travelers swear by raincoats or "windbreakers."

3 A nice dinner dress for women and a suit with tie for men is a good idea for shore visits to fine hotels and restaurants.

4 Luxury items like jewels or furs will most likely only cause consternation. The freighter line can't provide insurance, so the simplest thing is to keep your precious possessions at home.

5 The weather at sea can turn blustery. Hats (knitted watch caps are an excellent idea) come in handy, as do gloves and scarves.

A Lykes Lines freighter off Lake Charles, Louisiana, circa 1952

Photo by Elemore Morgan, Sr.

Other things you might need include:

1 Drug items. Bring plenty of vitamins, aspirins, antacids, and so forth. Americans especially assume everything's available at the ship's store, but that's not the case with freighters. Stock up on toothpaste, shampoo, mouthwash, and the like. The smartest traveler we know never leaves home without two thermometers, a heating pad, and a blood-pressure kit.

2 Reading materials. Freighters often provide books and magazines but perhaps not what you'll want. Now may be the time to settle in with *Bleak House* or another classic you've never read before. (Dare we suggest *Moby Dick* or *Lord Jim?*) Variety and scope are desirable, though, so pack a few "page-turners." Travel books about your destinations are essential.

3 Binoculars. Spotting wildlife—birds and fish—is a major freighter thrill, as is watching for other ships and, of course, shore!

4 Writing paper and notebooks. Some freighter travelers always bring a travel log to fill in on the way. Pack plenty of pens and pencils. Throw in a calendar, too.

5 An alarm clock.

Since shipping firms rarely insure passenger's belongings, experts strongly recommend that individual travelers take out insurance for all their baggage and personal effects, especially valuables.

Receiving mail while embarked on a voyage is tricky but can be done. Again, consult your travel or booking agent. Sometimes it's possible to get mail at ports of call if it's addressed to you and has your sailing date, the name of the vessel, and its final destination written on the envelope. Mark it to the attention of the freighter company's port agent.

A single room aboard a freighter

A freighter heads for port

The Lingo

Once you've embarked, you're in the company of seafaring people, and if you want to keep abreast of the goings-on aboard, this short glossary of terms will help:

Athwartship   moving from one side to the other
Beam   breadth of the ship at its widest part
Boatswain   (say bō'sun) senior officer in charge of crew
Bow   front of the ship
Bulkhead   wall
Knot   a nautical mile (6076.1 feet—about one-seventh longer than a land mile)
Ladders   stairs from one deck to another
Overhead   ceiling
Port   the left side
Starboard   the right side
Stern   rear of the ship

   Now . . . to the trips!

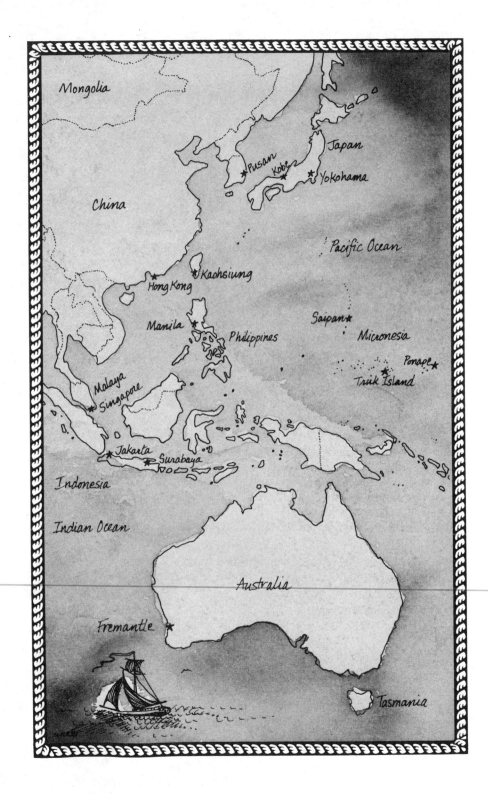

THREE

THE ORIENT

ORIENT LINE CRUISES

ORFORD   ORONSAY   ORONTES
20,000 TONS   20,000 TONS   20,000 TONS

THREE CRUISES IN MAY

2nd, 9th, 23rd

RHODES   ATHENS   MADEIRA

SEVEN SUMMER CRUISES

JUNE, JULY, AUGUST

NORWAY & NORTHERN CAPITALS

FARES FROM 20 GUINEAS

Punch 1930

Write for Programme: Anderson, Green & Co., Ltd., 5 Fenchurch Avenue, London, E.C.3

West End Offices : 14 Cockspur Street, S.W.1. & No. 1 Australia House, W.C.2

Advertisements lured the adventurous to freighter travel in England of 1930 as well as today, as shown in this page from *Punch* magazine. *Punch © 1931*

American President Lines

Oakland (California) to Japan via Okinawa and Hong Kong; Oakland to Singapore via Indonesia; and the Grab Bag

The American President Lines' fleet of freighters, all first class, includes five different types of ships designed for "roughing it in high style on the high seas." Special care has been taken in appointing these vessels, which resemble gracious hotels. Touches of elegance are everywhere—fine hardwood stairways with brass-accented balustrades, shimmering gossamer curtains at the windows, thick oriental carpets, artfully arranged chandeliers in the lounges, and the finest furniture. In the dining room, where passengers sit six at a table along with one of the ship's officers, there are cushy armchairs, pastel table linens, and luxurious china and silver. As for the staterooms, don't be surprised at teak inlaid floors, original oil paintings on the walls, and vases bursting with fresh flowers. Staterooms are spacious, complete with bathroom, bountiful closet and dresser space, as well as a dressing table, desk, couch, and lounge chairs.

As song and story promise, Pacific crossings feature trade winds softly blowing, clear skies, and unsurpassed sunsets. You'll soon settle in with your fellow travelers, never more than twelve a ship, for a casual hedonistic voyage during which your only scheduled activity is meals. Leisure activities aboard include deck games—American President boasts unusually well-situated and large deck areas—bridge or backgammon in the cardrooms, socializing in the lounge, or you can retire to your stateroom to enter the day's ruminations in your trip log or plan sightseeing jaunts at the next port of call.

One freighter travel aficionado, Earl Hatton, a New York writer whose love of the sea began during his childhood in southern Florida, worked as a crew mem-

American President Lines—The Orient

Type of Trip	From	To
cruise	Oakland (California)	Yokohama Kobe Pusan Okinawa Kaohsiung Hong Kong
cruise	Oakland	Guam Kaohsiung Hong Kong Singapore Jakarta Port Kelang Penang
"The Grab Bag" cruise	Various Pacific Northwest ports—ports vary; see text	Likely ports include: Pusan Singapore Malaysia India Pakistan

AHOY!

Free baggage limit is 350 pounds, excess at $.20 per pound.
No cars or pets can be taken along.
Children's fares: 1 to 11 years—half fare; 12 years and over—full fare.
Age limit—79 years.

This American President liner leaves a broad wake as it heads for sea. *American President Lines*

Fare	Duration of Trip	How Often Sails	Number of Passengers
$3600 (suite) $3180 (single) $2900 (double)	42 days	every 2 weeks	12
$4825 (suite) $4260 (single) $3880 (double)	56 days	every 2 weeks	12
$6930 (deluxe or single cabin) $6300 (double)	90 days	every 2 weeks	12

American President Lines
1950 Franklin Street
Oakland, California 94612
(415) 271-8000

ber on various freighters as a young man. Later, he became a frequent passenger. American President remains one of Earl's favorites because it supplies just the right mix of luxury and informality. "The staterooms are enormous! You could get lost . . . and it's so interesting to spend time with the officers. I can never get over their willingness to talk with passengers. Even if you feel like a fool, they're pleased to answer any question—whether it's how the radar works or what to see when you reach Yokohama."

Earl also enjoys being able to shop at ports along the way without fretting about how to bring home his purchases. "The cost of excess baggage comes to a pittance, so if you see a teak dining table and eight chairs in Okinawa, nothing stops you from buying them on the spot! One lady even bought a Pekingese dog. Now on what other mode of travel could you do *that*?"

An especially attractive feature of American President Lines is its so-called Grab Bag service, just the thing for folks who want to revel in what the line calls "one of the few remaining *real* freighter experiences." Years ago many other lines offered this kind of service, but almost none do today. Applicable only to C-5 cargo liners (the kind that carry large parcels of grain, tallow, machinery, newsprint, and other cargo items from the United States to the Far East), the Grab Bag trips adhere to *no* prede-

termined schedule or itinerary whatsoever. Demand for cargo service alone dictates the ship's comings and goings. If a shipment of teak in Singapore isn't quite ready to be loaded when you arrive, your ship will dock there and stay until the loading operation has been completed.

The C-5 ships used for Grab Bag tours spend quite a bit more time in each port than do scheduled cruises, affording passengers ample time for side trips while their ship docks. In one case a young woman from San Francisco disembarked in Hong Kong and became so entranced with the city and the surrounding countryside that, much to her family's chagrin, she stayed for several months!

Ports of call, too, vary considerably more for Grab Bag ships than on regularly scheduled trips, although to reiterate, flexibility is the name of the game in freighters, and ports are often changed and itineraries re-arranged. Sometimes a ship makes stops in only one or two countries, but the countries may include Japan, Korea, Taiwan, Singapore, Indonesia, India, Sri Lanka, or Bangladesh. Most often the ship calls at nine or ten countries. You get the idea. True to the term Grab Bag, almost nothing about the trip—sailing date, length of voyage, or ports of call—is hard and fast. Those who have traveled via American President's Grab Bag swear unpredictability makes for high adventure!

What about Grab Bag costs? As a result of this trip's flexibility, fares are based on an arbitrary trip length of ninety days. Rates as of this printing are $6300 for a standard double cabin, $6930 for a deluxe or single cabin. Should the voyage stretch out for over ninety days, American President Lines levies no additional fare. On the other hand, if the trip turns out to be shorter than ninety days, you'll be refunded at a rate of $70 per day for a double cabin and $77 for a deluxe or single cabin.

Hellenic Lines

New York to Calcutta via Sri Lanka, returning to Savannah (Georgia)

Hellenic Lines—home port, Piraeus, Greece—cruises to remote ports around the globe. The cruise we'll discuss here (other Hellenic trips will be outlined in appropriate sections later) to the Persian Gulf, Pakistan, and India is particularly enticing and very popular, so if it strikes your fancy, contact both Hellenic Lines and a freighter travel agent as soon as you finish reading this entry. Passenger booking specialists say vacancies on this cruise are hard to come by. (Also note carefully: the ship leaves from New York City but returns to Savannah, Georgia.)

In America, Hellenic operates out of New York, New Orleans, and Houston. Its fleet consists of forty-two ships with excellent accommodations for twelve passengers per ship. A stateroom for two on the *Hellenic Pride*, for example, features two comfortable beds, several armchairs, a desk, dressing table, dressers, and private bathroom—top-notch accoutrements for a freighter! The single stateroom (which, by the way, goes for the same price) is much the same, though smaller.

On each Hellenic boat there's a sizable dining room, lounge (or smoking room, as they call it), and pantry for between-meal snacks. Both open and enclosed deck areas assure continual access to fresh sea air, whether you relax in a deck chair with a good suspense novel or stroll out after dinner to stargaze.

Freighter specialists unanimously laud Hellenic's cuisine. The ship's cooks provide an astonishing array of authentic Greek repast—hors d'oeuvres, roast lamb, fine Retsina wines, stuffed grape leaves, and sumptuous desserts such as the sweet custard called galactaburico—as well as French specialties such as boeuf bourguignon, soufflés, assorted cheeses, and desserts. Hellenic's customers invariably return from their cruises praising the chefs.

On this New York to Calcutta trip, plan on spending three to four days in each port. If, however, you know beforehand that you'd like a longer stay in any particular city on the itinerary, mention this when you contact the booking agent. Arrangements can often be made to lengthen your sojourn in, say, Bombay by allowing you to pick up the next Hellenic ship that cruises through, usually within about two weeks.

This cruise takes you to remarkable ports. Few ships, freighters, or luxury liners call at Persian Gulf ports, so Hellenic's trip provides you with a rare opportunity. After the Atlantic crossing, you sail around the Cape of Good Hope into the Indian Ocean and north to the Arabian Sea. The first port as you pass from the Gulf of Oman into the Persian Gulf is Dubai, perhaps the most vital seaport in the United Arab Republic—and in today's world no one has to be reminded of that country's geographic and economic importance.

The ship continues up the Persian Gulf, putting in at Bahrain, an island off Saudi Arabia that functions as the country's port. Next your tour of the Persian Gulf moves to Kuwait, that notorious oil-rich nation where every facet of life, as you will witness firsthand, reflects its enormous newfound wealth. Without a doubt, your stay in Kuwait will be enlightening.

Hellenic's cruise proceeds out of the Persian Gulf into the Arabian Sea to call on Karachi, Pakistan. (So far, by the way, you've visited three Far Eastern countries.) After several days to explore Karachi, you're in for an even greater thrill as the ship sails down the west coast of India, stopping first at Daman, a small port near Bombay. Bombay itself is a city virtually exploding with twentieth-century commerce superimposed on a

Hellenic Lines freighter *Hellenic Lines*

Hellenic Lines—Middle East, Far East

Type of Trip	From	To
cruise	New York—returning to Savannah (Georgia)	Dubai Bahrain Daman Kuwait Karachi Bombay Colombo Calcutta
cruise	New York—returning to Savannah	same ports

AHOY!

Free baggage limit is 25 cubic feet, 13 cubic feet for half fares. Ask Hellenic for excess baggage rate.

Cars can be taken on certain trips as regular freight with 25% discount. Pets are permitted with veterinarian's certificate and rabies inoculation certificate at $350 for dogs and $200 for cats.

Children's fares: under 1 year—free; 1 to 12 years—half fare; over 12 years—full fare.

Valid certificates of smallpox and cholera vaccination are required for these cruises.

Since no doctor is aboard, passengers 65 years of age or over must submit doctor's certificate of good health.

---

culture dating back nearly 5000 years. While you're there, you'll undoubtedly be tempted by its celebrated goods, brassware, and wood carvings. India's export economy is thriving since the demand for its goods—coffee, jute, ores, tobacco, rubber, and tea, in addition to the previously listed items—grows each year.

After leaving Bombay, your ship steams down the west coast and around the tip of Indian to the island of Sri Lanka (formerly Ceylon). Consider yourself a member of an elite, blessed community of travelers the second you set foot on Sri Lanka, an exquisite country indeed. You'll dock in Colombo, the capital and major port where products such as tea, rubber (Sri Lanka ranks second only to India in the export of rubber), spices, and precious stones are dispatched around the globe. Although Sri Lanka lies near the equator, sea breezes will keep you cool. Be sure to tour the tea plantations, the ebony and sandalwood forests, the rubber plantations, and

Fare	Duration of Trip	How Often Sails	Number of Passengers
$5500	150–170 days	twice monthly	12
$5700	190 days	twice monthly	12

Hellenic Lines
39 Broadway
New York, New York 10006
(212) 482-5694

Hellenic Lines
1314 Texas Avenue
Houston, Texas 77002
(713) 224-8607

Hellenic Lines
2812 International Trade Mart
New Orleans, Louisiana 70130
(504) 581-2825

Hellenic Lines
Filonos Street 61/65
Piraeus, Greece
417-1541

the sapphire and ruby mines. Also, the delicate wood carvings of Sri Lanka's mosques are renowned among Moslem countries.

Before sailing homeward, your ship moves up the east coast of India into the Bay of Bengal for its final stop at Calcutta, a city as large as Bombay but different enough to make it well worth touring.

From there you move full speed ahead, back around Africa, across the Atlantic, and into your final port, Savannah, Georgia. In all, Hellenic's India trip may leave you anxious to embark again . . . right away!

Knutsen Line

San Francisco to Fremantle via Hong Kong and Singapore, returning to Vancouver, British Columbia

Knutsen Line specializes in freighters that cross the Pacific Ocean to the Orient and Western Australia. Its vessels are commodious yet cozy with a large lounge, dining saloon, lots of deck space, and a swimming pool. A maximum of twelve passengers per ship stay in four double and four single cabins, all with private baths.

But for all the comfort of the ships, it's Knutsen's itinerary that takes center stage. You leave San Francisco, stop in Hong Kong, Manila, Singapore, and Fremantle, and sometimes Kobe and Yokohama as well. As is common with freighters, the precise itinerary usually remains indefinite until virtually the last minute. Chances are you'll hit at least five of the six ports on Knutsen's list; however, the order is likely to be jumbled. For a further venturesome twist, all Knutsen ships return to Vancouver, British Columbia, an extraordinarily delightful city.

If you talk directly to a Knutsen agent, be prepared to hear: "We're not in the cruise business." But don't worry or be put off. This simply means that a separate application must be made for your return trip. In other words, you can't automatically book round-trip passage. Thus we've listed the itinerary on the accompanying chart as separate one-way trips, though you can, in effect, make it a cruise. Schedules on Knutsen fluctuate, so rather than encounter disappointed or inconvenienced travelers, the line insists on processing eastbound and westbound applications individually. Here's an excellent reason to use one of the freighter agents we've recommended at the end of the book—just to make doubly sure no problems occur.

An anthropology professor in her early fifties who'd heard lively reports from colleagues about freighter trips to foreign shores made this Knutsen voyage at a

The *M.S. John Bakke* of Knutsen Line pulling into San Francisco *Knutsen Line*

pivotal point in her life. The previous year, in one fell swoop, she resigned from her job, separated from her husband, and booked passage thinking that a melancholy woman "of a certain age" would profit from a long migration. Friends and relatives immediately banded together to offer her companionship, country homes, money—*anything* to dissuade her from spending time on "some dreary boat." Mrs. X. became nervous. Was she doing the right or wrong thing?

In retrospect, to hear Mrs. X's descriptions, the trip became a magical, curative right of passage. From the moment she set sail from San Francisco, the serenity of the sea provided respite from her gaggle of well-meaning but annoying friends, not to mention fretting family. "My days came and went in absolute harmony," she reports. "Never once did I long for home or question my decision. Each morning after breakfast I'd sit on deck, knitting and sipping tea until lunch. Several of the passengers were near my age, sensitive, friendly— not that they pressured me or interfered in my need for solitude. For the first time in my life I could be anonymous—nobody's wife, mother, pal. Now I know why freighter travelers find it addictive! I came home a new woman!"

★ ★

Knutsen Line—Orient

Type of Trip	From	To
cruise	San Francisco, returning to Vancouver	Hong Kong Manila Singapore Fremantle
one way one way one way one way	San Francisco—all trips return to Vancouver, British Columbia	Hong Kong Manila Singapore Fremantle

AHOY!

Free baggage limit is 350 pounds, not counting hand baggage. Ask Knutsen for excess baggage rates.

Cars can be taken at prevailing tariff rates. Pets are not permitted.

Children's fares: under 1 year—quarter fare; 1 to 12 years—half fare; 12 years and up—full fare.

Passengers must show proof of smallpox vaccination within three years. Also, two cholera shots are required.

Knutsen Line will not accept people over 70 years of age.

Here are a few capsule descriptions of the inordinately attractive ports along Knutsen's route:

Manila, on the superb tropical island of Luzon, largest of the 7100 islands that make up the Philippines, gives you a chance to observe the merger of Spanish, American, and native Filipino cultures. Historically, Manila played a key role in World War II, when Americans and Filipinos remained imprisoned by the Japanese for several years in the ruins of the old Spanish dungeon at Fort Santiago. You'll want to peruse the colonial section of town and drive through the countryside of rice paddies, coconut palms, and banana plantations, past the barrios, or villages built on stilts to withstand violent weather and floods. Other musts to see: Tagaytay Ridge, a 2000-foot-high promontory overlooking Lake Taal, the crater of an extinct volcano that contains yet another volcano said to be the smallest volcano in the world.

The extraordinary island of Penang off the west coast of the Malay Peninsula is a voluptuous paradise redolent with cloves, nutmeg, and other products of its profuse fruit and nut groves. Its natives—Malay, Chinese, Indian, and some blends thereof—have created a unique culture, as testified by such monuments as the Snake Temple, built in 1850. You'll

Fare	Duration of Trip	How Often Sails	Number of Passengers
$2250; 2300	32 days	twice monthly	12
$1175; 1225	17 days	twice monthly	12
$1530; 1580	21 days	twice monthly	
$1700; 1750	26 days	twice monthly	
$2250; 2300	32 days	twice monthly	

Knutsen Line
Bakke Steamship Corp.
650 California Street
San Francisco, California 94108
(415) 433-4200

also see rare tropical vegetation on display in a series of botanical gardens. Also of special interest is the Temple of the Reclining Buddha in George Town, the third largest temple in the world.

Those who have traveled with Knutsen invariably remark on the fascinating contrast between cities like Penang on the one hand and Fremantle on the other. A major port city on the western coast of Australia, about a week's sail from Manila—less from Penang—Fremantle is a small, simple town of wooden Victorian houses replete with the typical gingerbread trim. It is encircled by forests of gigantic hardwood trees, and farther to the south are numerous caves where not so many years ago paleontologists discovered fossils of giant marsupials. Australia's bizarre life and vegetation are well-known, and Fremantle offers good examples of both. Certain wildflowers in the Fremantle area, in fact, are exported around the world. Finally, Perth, another charming Australian city, can be reached easily in a matter of hours and would make a worthwhile side-trip while you're docked in Fremantle.

All this and Japan too!

Lykes Lines

San Francisco to Hong Kong via Indonesia, Japan, and Hawaii; San Francisco, Seattle, or Portland to Yokohama via Honolulu, returning to Long Beach (California); New Orleans to Yokohama via Bangkok and Indonesia

Ready for the junket of a lifetime? Lykes Lines' cruise to the Pacific, Southeast Asia, and the Orient combines the ecstasy of a Pacific crossing with tours of some of the most interesting, beautiful, and exotic cities in the world. More about the route below, but first some background on Lykes.

The majority of the Lykes fleet of forty-four freighters—classified in five classes: Pacer, Andes, Clipper, Pride, and "Roll-On, Roll-Off"— carry twelve passengers per voyage, although two, the Pride and the Clipper classes, accept only eight. All cabins on Lykes ships are doubles. Thus if you're traveling alone and don't wish to pay extra to have the cabin to yourself, be prepared to bunk-in with a newfound friend. Lykes also has a number of spacious "preferred staterooms" that are distributed on a first-come, first-served basis. Move quickly to make reservations should you want one of these. But no matter if your stateroom is "preferred" or shared, it's situated outside and has a private bathroom.

Because the Lykes ships vary a good deal, it's important to familiarize yourself with each type. The "Roll-On, Roll-Off" vessels, a special category of ship with six two-berth cabins, tend to move swiftly from port to port. In fact, your time in any given port may be limited to as little as eight to twenty-four hours. If, however, you're a natural-born seafarer, these ships are just the ticket, since a trip on them makes sight-seeing a definite second to drifting around the Pacific. Be sure to tell your travel agent whether you want "Roll-On, Roll-Off" or conventional service.

Accommodations, too, differ slightly from ship to ship. Those of the Pacer, Andes, and "Roll-On, Roll-Off" classes have separate passenger lounges, while the Clipper's large lounge area is shared with the ship's officers. On the Pride class, the dining room doubles as a lounge between meal hours.

On all Lykes ships, passengers dine with the officers, making for lively, informative table talk. Meals—hearty American cuisine expertly prepared—are served from 7:40 to 8:30 for breakfast, from 11:40 to 12:30 for lunch, and from 5:10 to 6:00 for supper. Each day the kitchen posts the menu so passengers can make their selections and notify the staff. In the evening, snacks are served from or in the pantry.

As you can see from the chart, Lykes also offers the option of booking one-way reservations to practically any port on its cuisine circuits. The plus here is that you can act as an independent explorer. The tricky part can be coordinating your return trip. We suggest, therefore, that you discuss your plans carefully with one of the freighter travel specialists listed at the end of the book.

Now glance down the itinerary of a Lykes voyage, and we will bewitch you with tales of some of these superlative ports. Jakarta and Surabaja, both part of Indonesia—a Southeast Asian country consisting of more than 13,600 islands along the equator—are situated on the island of Java, a fantasy island of tropical rain forests, tigers, crocodiles, elephants, and volcanoes juxtaposed with the scene of a Dutch colonization that left neat ribbons of European-style houses along Jakarta's pristine canals.

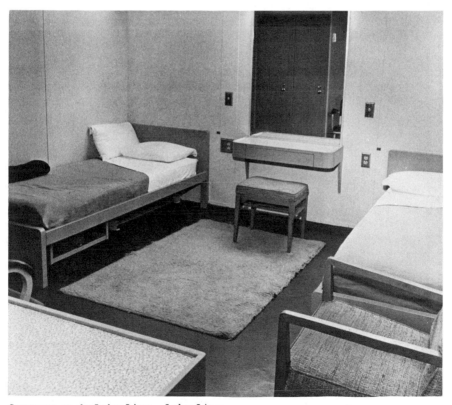

Stateroom on the Lykes Lines   *Lykes Lines*

Lykes Lines—The Orient

Type of Trip	From	To
cruise	San Francisco	Taiwan Manila Singapore Jakarta, Surabaja Hong Kong Taiwan Kobe, Yokohama Honolulu
cruise	San Francisco, Seattle, or Portland—returning to Long Beach (California)	Yokohama Kaohsiung Pusan Kobe, Yokohama Honolulu Long Beach
one way one way one way one way one way one way one way	San Francisco	Taiwan Manila Singapore Jakarta Surabaja Kobe Honolulu
cruise	New Orleans	Kobe, Yokohama Pusan Hong Kong Taiwan Singapore Bangkok Jakarta

AHOY!

Free baggage limit is 350 pounds. Ask Lykes Lines for excess baggage charges.
Pets, cars, and campers are allowed aboard. Ask agent for rates.
Children's fares: 1 to 11 years—half fare; over 11—full fare.
Smallpox and cholera inoculations are required for all cruises.
Age limit: Passengers over 70 years may not apply for passage.

Fare	Duration of Trip	How Often Sails	Number of Passengers
$3600	80 days	5 to 6 times monthly	12 or 8 (see entry)
$2050	32 days	3 to 4 times monthly	12 or 8
$965	13 days	3 to 4 times monthly	12 or 8
$1120	21 days		
$1190	35 days		
$1345	30 days		
$1420	26 days		
$965	50 days		
$345	28 days		
$2400	70–80 days	every 3 months	12 or 8

Lykes Lines
300 Poydras Street
New Orleans, Louisiana 70130
(504) 523-6611

Lykes Lines
Melrose Building
Houston, Texas 77002

Lykes Lines
320 California Street
San Francisco, California 94104

This photograph, taken in 1939, shows the deck of the *S.S. Mormactide. Kramer*

Most Indonesian people are Malays whose ancestors came from the mainland about 5000 years ago. (Some Arabs, Chinese, and Papuans live there today as well.) Luckily for tourists, the most highly developed arts in Indonesia are those of the Javanese. Its dancers and puppet shows of breathtaking artistry and strangeness can be seen at specially arranged performances. They are accompanied by an orchestra consisting of metal gongs with flutes, gambangs (instruments similar to xylophones), double-ended drums, and rebabs (two-stringed instruments played like cellos).

Your visit to Java can also be enriched by touring its many extraordinary Hindu and Buddhist temples. Famous Indonesian crafts, all of which can be purchased by visitors, include batik (a process of waxing and dying, now fairly well-known in the United States, which creates exquisitely colored and patterned fabrics), puppets, and carved daggers called krises. In addition, Indonesian sports such as cockfights, oxen races, bullfights, and pentjak (a fascinating amalgam of dance and self-defense) can be observed throughout Java.

Jakarta retains much Dutch architectural influence. A colony of stilt houses on the outskirts of a town, resembling a miniature Amsterdam, is common. The botanical gardens here offer a seductive array of rare flowers and plants, including the rafflesia, the largest flower in the world, and the Victoria water lily, with leaves often more than five feet in diameter. Equally unique, exotic, and outstanding is Indonesian cuisine. So resolve to have a meal at one of Jakarta's leading hotels.

Your ship also docks at the Indonesian city of Surabaja, whose major sights are the Kajoon flower market, endless stalls of rare blooms; the city zoo, Home of the Komodo dragon; and the East Javanese Kuda Kepang dancers. Possible side excursions (by train or plane) could include Jokjakarta in southern Java, famed for its batik factories, silversmiths, and the sumptuous Ambarrukmo Palace Hotel; Kraton, Palace of the Sultan of Jokja; and Borobudur, sanctuary of the Mahayana Buddhist faith. Another excursion to consider is a ferry ride to the island of Madura for the notorious Karapan Sapi bull races. If you go, plan to take in the dancing ceremony that precedes the races, as well as the traditional Indonesian buffet that follows.

Freighter of the Lykes Lines *Lykes Lines*

Naura Pacific Line

San Francisco to Micronesia via Honolulu

According to Pearl Hoffman of Pearl's Freighter Tips in Great Neck, New York (see list of freighter agents at end of book), nothing beats a cruise on Naura Pacific Line. And Pearl knows! She provides travelers with inside information, not to mention T.L.C.—obtains reservations, keeps up with ever-changing departure schedules, and even finds a hotel in New York if you're from out of town. When asked about the Micronesia cruise, Pearl rolls her huge brown eyes, sighs longingly, and says the voyage is divine.

Naura Pacific's beautiful, luxurious ship, the M. V. *Enna G,* a cargo

The cargoliner *Enna G* of the Naura Pacific Line sails approximately every six weeks from San Francisco, via Honolulu, to Majuro, Ponape, Truk, and Saipan. *Naura Pacific Line*

liner, carries up to 100 passengers from San Francisco across the blue Pacific to Honolulu, then on to Micronesia, combining perhaps the finest ship in the freighter class with a superb Pacific crossing that ends in an island paradise.

First, the *Enna G.* Its promenade deck consists, in the aft, of an outdoor sports deck, a swimming pool, and an adjacent glassed-in bar overlooking the pool area. On one side of the deck is a glass-enclosed promenade and verandah, ideal for daytime or nighttime lounging. Close by are a writing room and library. The ship's immense dining room takes up almost the entire starboard side of the promenade deck, and in the bow there's a lounge the width of the ship's beam, complete with dance floor where each evening after supper a small orchestra plays. Staterooms are situated on the main and upper decks.

Fans of the *Enna G* are always enthusiastic about its interior design. In the light-bathed, plant-filled lounge, for instance, shocking-pink armchairs surround gaming tables arranged near an endless expanse of windows that command a panoramic view of the sea, creating a room conducive to merriment. The subtly-lit dining room, on the other hand, has a more austere, men's social club ambience with paneled mahogany walls and armchairs upholstered in warm chocolate brown. Windows abound, but gossamer curtains create a restful atmosphere.

Yet another design scheme applies in the staterooms, which tend to vibrant primary colors—azure blue, flaming orange, lime green—with coordinated plushy carpets and floral print curtains at the portholes. All stateroom furniture—chairs, desks, dressers, mirrors—is of the finest polished teak and rosewood.

With you contentedly ensconced in a deck chair on the verandah of the *Enna G*, the Micronesia cruise commences as the ship steams out of San Francisco harbor bound for Honolulu. You'll have several days to enjoy the pleasures of this festive, sophisticated city, a definite resort capital. Meander along famed Waikiki Beach with its world-class surfers, then dress up in sports finery to visit Honolulu's downtown nightclubs, as glittery as those of Las Vegas yet more exotic.

After another few days aboard the *Enna G*, you'll call at Majuro, dubbed the "pearl of the Pacific" by Robert Louis Stevenson. This atoll stretches for thirty-five miles, with an unbelievable blue lagoon bordered by white beaches. It's the island paradise you've dreamed of. Trade winds blow, the tiny towns of thatch-roof cottages are rustically perfect, and the snorkeling, fishing, and scuba diving couldn't be better!

From Majuro you sail to the island of Ponape, the Garden Isle of Micronesia. The main city, Kolonia, is situated 2000 feet above sea level and has a constant cap of puffy white clouds hovering over its surrounding mountains. All around are dense tropical forests, tumbling waterfalls, and quiet clear pools for swimming or Narcissus-like gazing. There is much to see, so plan on a busy two or three days. Visit the Venetian-type canals built by

Naura Pacific Line—The Orient, South Pacific

Type of Trip	From	To
Micronesia cruise	San Francisco	Honolulu Majuro Ponape Truk Saipan

AHOY!

Free baggage limit is 500 pounds. Check with Naura Pacific for excess baggage charges.

Naura Lines is unable to carry either cars or pets.

Children's fares: under 1 year—free; 1 to 3 years—quarter fare; 3 to 12 years—half fare.

Age limit: Naura Pacific reserves the right to refuse passage to persons with conditions that might preclude a long ocean voyage. Any illness or disability or special treatment must be reported to the line in advance. Persons over 65 years of age must submit a doctor's certificate attesting to fitness for such travel.

Stateroom on the *Enna G*. All *Enna G* staterooms have outside exposure and are air conditioned. *Naura Pacific Line*

Fare	Duration of Trip	How Often Sails	Number of Passengers
$3800	39–41 days	every 6 weeks	100

North American Maritime Agencies
100 California Street
San Francisco, California 94111
(415) 981-0343

the Saudeleurs 700 years ago and the Polynesian village of Porakiet, a market community selling arts and crafts from throughout Micronesia.

Next stop is Truk, where the Japanese Imperial Navy anchored its fleet during World War II in the forty-mile-wide Truk lagoon, the world's largest. Over 100 ships, planes, and submarines destroyed by U.S. attacks in the 1944 siege lie submerged there. Tours of the area thus provide a glimpse into recent history. All the while, the essence of South Pacific natural wonders surround you—clear lagoons and enticing jungle vegetation.

On to Saipan, island headquarters of the Congress of Micronesia, where one side of the island consists of a rocky landscape with tidal pools, plateaus, and cliffs, while the other has wide stretches of sandy beaches sloping down to the reef. Most tourists who come to Saipan opt for a glass-bottomed boat trip to view the extensive coral and marine life. For a final diversion before you sail on, trek (or hire a boat and float) out to the north end of the island, an uninhabited area of thick rain forest, caves, cliffs, and the famous Blue Grotto, an enormous volcanic cavern connected by underground passageways to the Pacific Ocean beyond.

Panama Canal

Curaçao

La Guaira

Puerto Cabello

Buenaventura

Guayaquil

Fortaleza

Callao

Salvador

Pacific Ocean

Antofagasta

Rio de Janeiro

Santos

Porto Alegre

Valparaiso

Rio Grande

Buenos Aires

Montevideo

Atlantic Ocean

Strait of Magellan

MARSH

SOUTH AMERICA

A *Life* magazine advertisement, 1911   *Hamburg-American Line*

Delta Steamship Lines

New York to west coast of South America via Panama Canal ("The Explorer" cruise and "The Conquistador" cruise); also Los Angeles (etc.) to west and east coasts of South America ("The Grand Circle" cruise)

Freighter travel cognoscenti invariably agree that Delta, which has specialized in cruises around the Americas for over 120 years, ranks among the classiest lines. Delta claims that traveling aboard one of its ships is like being a guest on a private yacht—and the comparison is apt. Although certain Delta cruise liners can accommodate up to one hundred passengers, the service and facilities are such that you can find a cozy, private corner when you're in a contemplative mood or join the others if it's conviviality you're after.

A Delta Liner bound from New York to South America   *Delta Steamship Lines*

Delta Steamship Lines—South America

Type of Trip	From	To
"The Explorer" cruise	New York	Panama Buenaventura Guayaquil Callao Valparaiso Panama Canal
"The Conquistador" cruise	Los Angeles, San Francisco, Tacoma, or Vancouver	Manzanillo Balboa Cartagena La Guaira Rio de Janeiro Valparaiso Callao
"The Grand Circle" cruise	Los Angeles, San Francisco, Tacoma, or Vancouver	Manzanillo Balboa Panama Canal Cartagena Puerto Cabello La Guaira Salvador Rio de Janeiro Santos Rio Grande Buenos Aires Strait of Magellan Valparaiso Callao Guayaquil
one way	Los Angeles	La Guaira
one way	Los Angeles	Rio de Janeiro
one way	Los Angeles	Valparaiso

AHOY!

Free baggage limit is 500 pounds, 250 per half fare, excess at $.03 per pound.
Cars and pets are not accepted.
Children's fares: under 3 years—free; 3 to 11 years—half fare; 11 and up—full fare.
All passengers must have valid smallpox vaccination issued within three years of
   sailing date. Check with Delta for further vaccination requirements.
Passengers 65 to 79 years of age must present a doctor's certificate of good health
   issued within three months of sailing date. Passengers 80 years or older are
   not accepted.

Fare	Duration of Trip	How Often Sails	Number of Passengers
$2940 (double) $3430 (single)	42 days	every week	12
$8155 (double) $9485 (single) $14,245 (suite)	54 days	every week	12
$14,245 (deluxe) to $7510 (see text)	65 days	every 2 weeks	100
$2195	14 weeks	every 2 weeks	100
$3890 (double) $4530 (single)	28 days	every 2 weeks	100
$6260 (double) $7280 (single)	42 days	every 2 weeks	100

Delta Steamship Lines
1 World Trade Center
New York, New York 10048
(212) 432-4700

Delta Steamship Lines
1 Market Plaza
San Francisco, California 94106
(415) 777-8300

Delta offers two different types of service on two different types of ships—cargo liners and cruise liners. From the East Coast, cargo liners carrying up to twelve passengers travel down the west coast of South America. These ships consist of three decks where you can sit, bask in the sun, walk, or ocean-gaze. In addition, there is an observation area over the bridge. Besides the spacious staterooms, each of which is located amidships, there are numerous lounges and a comfortable dining room. On Delta cargo liners, all staterooms have a private bath, wall-to-wall carpeting, individually controlled air conditioning, and loads of drawer and closet space, not to mention large windows. If you consult the accompanying table, note that both "The Explorer" cruise and "The Conquistador" cruise are made by cargo liner ships.

Cruise liner service for "The Grand Circle" cruise from the West Coast (Los Angeles, San Francisco, Tacoma, or Vancouver) is quite another story. These ships are larger and more opulent. As the accompanying pictures illustrate, Delta cruise liners consist of five decks with staterooms available on all but the observation deck and the promenade deck. Since prices vary for staterooms on "The Grand Circle" cruise, they are categorized into six types of rooms, from the grandest to the simplest:

Room Type A: Outside room with either two single beds and sofa bed, or double bed and sofa bed. Shower or tub-shower.

Room Type 1: Outside room with two single beds or double bed, some with upper wall bed or sofa bed. Shower or tub-shower.

Room Type 2: Outside room with sofa bed, folding lower wall bed, folding upper wall bed. Tub-shower.

Room Type 3: Outside room with sofa bed, folding lower wall bed. Some with folding upper wall bed as well. Shower.

Room Type 4: Outside room with one sofa bed, folding upper wall bed. Shower.

Room Type 5: Inside room with one sofa bed, folding upper wall bed. Shower.

Now let's look at each deck, going from the top to the bottom. On the observation deck, which is mostly an open expanse of space, you'll find the most panoramic view of the ocean. Thus many passengers go there with

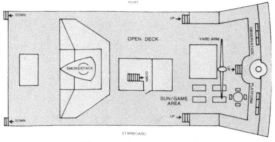

Observation deck on a Delta liner

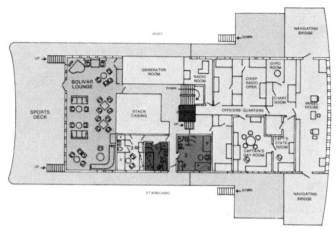

Bridge deck on a Delta liner

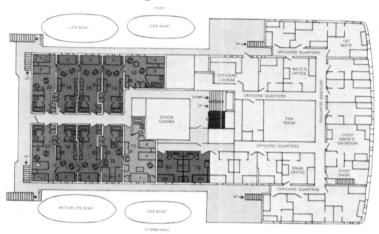

Sun deck on a Delta liner

binoculars or equipped with a deck chair and a companion. Directly below on the bridge deck, you'll find the officers' quarters, the navigating bridge, the wheelhouse, and the posh Bolivar Lounge, which overlooks both an outdoor sports deck and three staterooms: one Type 4 at $7090 double (each), $8865 single; one Type 3 at $7620 double, $10,480 single; one Type 1 at $9975 double, $19,945 single.

On the sun deck, one deck below, you'll find one Type A room at $14,245 double, $28,495 single; four Type 1 rooms (same prices as above); four Type 2 rooms at $8605 double, $15,940 single; and one Type A room at $14,245 double, $28,495 single. It's also possible to reserve one of four deluxe suites on this deck, which become available when the adjoining rooms have been purchased at full fare. Consult a freighter travel agent or Delta for exact prices.

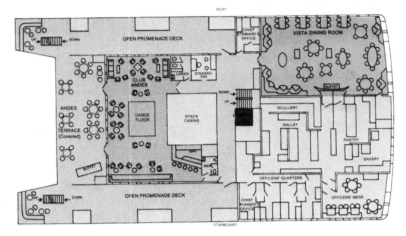

Delta promenade deck

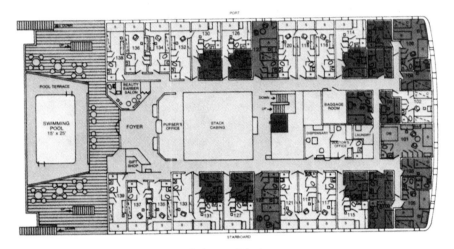

Delta pool deck

One deck below the promenade deck is the covered Andes Terrace with a fine view off the ship's stern, two open promenade decks, a large cabaret area with dance floor, the Club Andes cocktail lounge, and the Vista dining room with buffet area.

Directly below is the pool deck with a variety of room types in every price category, though mostly Type 3. (A double in the Type 3 category costs $7620; a single, $10,480.) For students or Spartan folk, there are thrifty staterooms (Type 5) on the pool deck, all situated inside without a porthole, priced at $7510. Other facilities on the pool deck include the swimming pool, its terrace, the doctor's office, laundry, hairdresser, and gift shop.

Now let's take a closer look at the itinerary of another Delta cruise—"The Explorer"—which takes you on a seven-week jaunt to outstanding ports along the west coast of South America. Since (as you might expect) some Delta stops are unscheduled, spontaneity being the *sine qua non* of freighter travel, count on surprises, particularly during your passage through the Caribbean.

The first official port of call is the Panama Canal, but before entering the canal, you may stop at Cristobal, a free port city with enticing bargains on native handicrafts. But, if you've never seen the canal itself, your greatest thrill comes as your ship passes through the Gatun Locks, bordered by lush, island-studded Gatun Lake, then Gaillard Cut and even more locks, all components of the Panama Canal complex.

After the canal you move on to other ports on the north coast of South America. Your first stop is Barranquilla, Colombia, where, thanks to a special Delta plan, you can disembark for either the ship's scheduled port time or longer. Passengers often choose to linger in Colombia, taking side trips to the cities of Santa Marta, San Andrés, Medellin, or Bogota (the latter two are high in the Andes Mountains), or perhaps to the colonial city of Cartagena. Delta Lines will be pleased to arrange a flight to enable you to rejoin the ship at ports farther south.

A word of advice: Due to the changeable climate on South America's west coast, take along both lightweight clothing for tropical and subtropical climates and heavier apparel for temperate zones. Should you plan to visit Peru, warm clothes and sturdy shoes are essential.

(From May to August, Delta provides a complimentary shore excursion in each South American port of call—a wonderful bonus!)

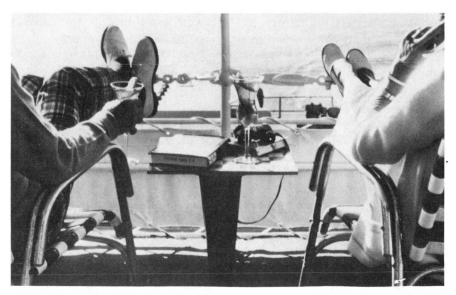

Drinks on deck, bound for South America

Ivaran Lines

Philadelphia, Baltimore, Charleston, Savannah, Miami to east coast of South America, returning to New Bedford (Massachusetts) or New York City

A recent addition to the freighter-passenger family is Ivaran Lines, which started as a freighter-only service in 1902 when Norwegian Ivar Anton Christensen purchased his first ship, the *S.S. Modesta*. Since then the Ivaran retinue has grown, until now the house flag and funnel stack with the white C on a field of red are familiar in all the world's major shipping ports. Currently, Ivaran's focus is trade between the United States, Argentina, and Brazil, and since 1978 two of its modern container vessels feature high-quality passenger accommodations.

The two vessels, the MS *Salvador* and the MS *Santa Fe*, both built in 1978, primarily purvey cargo. Their second aim, however, is first-class passenger service. Both ships are fully air-conditioned, with a dining room, a sitting room, a bar with television, and a swimming pool—all for up to twelve passengers housed in four double cabins and four single cabins, each with a private bathroom. A pleasant, polyglot crew, whose

An Ivaran freighter *Ivaran Lines*

The Bay of Guanabara, Rio de Janeiro *Sociedade Anonima Viagens International*

languages include English, consider it their personal duty to make each voyage a pleasurable, interesting one for their guests.

Ivaran's routing to South America starts along the eastern coast of America, embarking from Philadelphia with stops at Baltimore, Charleston, Savannah, and Miami. The advantage to prospective passengers is that you can arrange to begin the cruise from the port closest to your home, unless like so many travelers, you want to take this opportunity to see American port cities from the shore! Freighter travel agents report that their clients often come home as enthused about putting in at, say, Savannah, Georgia, for a day or two as they are about Rio de Janeiro.

At any rate, your Ivaran ship skirts the Bahamas, circles the West Indies, and steams south to Rio de Janeiro, the first foreign port. From there the ports are Santos, Buenos Aires, Montevideo, Pôrto Alegre, Rio Grande, Paranaguá, Santos again, Bahia, and Fortaleza. The cruise ends at either New Bedford, Massachusetts, or New York.

Ivaran Lines—South America

Type of Trip	From	To
cruise	Philadelphia, Baltimore, Charleston, Savannah, Miami—returning to New Bedford, Massachusetts or New York City	Rio de Janeiro Santos Buenos Aires Montevideo Porto Alegre Rio Grande Paranaguá Bahia Fortaleza

AHOY!

Free baggage limit is 40 cubic feet. Excess at $2.50 per cubic foot.
Pets are not accepted. Cars can be taken along.
Children's fares: under 12—half fare.
Age limit: No person 75 years of age or over may make the trip. Those 65 must
provide a doctor's certificate of good health.

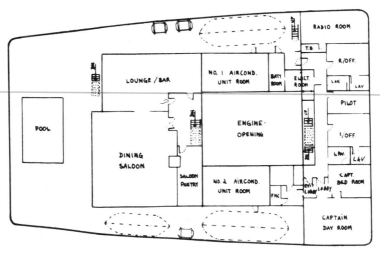

Boat deck on an Ivaran liner   *Ivaran Lines*

Fare	Duration of Trip	How Often Sails	Number of Passengers
$3500 (double) $4000 (single)	50 days	twice monthly	12

Ivaran Lines
United States Navigation Inc.
17 Battery Place
New York, New York 10004
(212) 269-6000

A/S Ivarans Rederi
Tollbugaten 11
Oslo 1, Norway
42-98-37

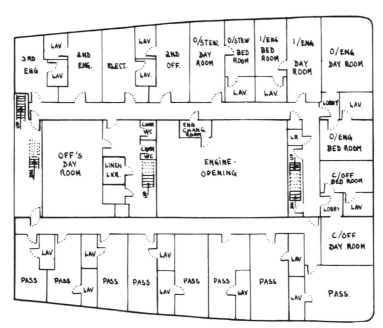

Passenger deck on an Ivaran liner   *Ivaran Lines*

Lykes Lines

New Orleans to the west coast of South America, cruise or one way to all ports

If you read about the Lykes Lines' trip to the Far East in Chapter 3, you already know something about this worldwide company. If not, you'll find a summary of vital information at the end of this chapter.

Lykes offers trips along the west coast of South America with seven possible stops or one-way passage to any of these ports and several more. While the east coast of South America regularly attracts tourists to cities like Rio de Janeiro and Buenos Aires, the sights and sounds of Chile and Peru are less familiar. Indeed not many conventional cruise ships venture there. And of the few that do, Lykes is among the most economical.

Also, Lykes encourages enterprising meanderings within your itinerary. Instead of staying aboard for the entire cruise, hop off for short jaunts or travel point to point. Lykes will gladly help you formulate your own tailor-made plans. The payoff is freedom to roam the Andes, follow the conquistadores' trails, climb the heights of Machu Picchu, or just loll on the deserted beaches of Colombia or Ecuador until you're ready to return to civilization via the comfort of your Lykes ship.

The face of Marta Nivon, a New York sweater designer, lights up as she reminisces about a South American trip she took on a Lykes ship some years ago with her parents and sister. "We kids were fussed over and pampered. The crew showed us around, told us everything about navigation, which flattered us, but what we really loved was helping them with the dishes. Here we were, two little girls, stirring huge cauldrons of soup,

The officers' dining salon, where passengers join the ship's officers for meals *Ivaran Lines*

drying glassware. At the end of the trip, the crew gave me this very pretty pocketbook for helping them in the kitchen! My sister, who was quite a bit older, got another kind of gift—the first mate had a crush on her and they started to go out on dates! He was South American, very nice, but, of course, my mother chaperoned them!"

In her most fetching story, Marta describes the party the crew gave when the ship crossed the Equator. "In homage to Neptune, god of the sea, they served a huge dinner, roast suckling pig, with loads of champagne. Everybody, passengers, officers, and crew, danced. When I think back on it, I giggle, but this is the part I don't think I liked too much at the time, You see, anyone who hadn't crossed the equator before got doused with a bucket of water, and on that trip I was among those who got doused. Someone in the crew just came right over and poured water on us—then we got a certificate. I've still got it framed on my wall!"

Lykes Lines—South America

Type of Trip	From	To
cruise	New Orleans	Cartagena Cristobal Balboa Buenaventura Guayaquil Callao Matarani
cruise	New Orleans	Cartagena Cristobal Balboa Buenaventura Guayaquil Antofagasta Valparaiso
one way one way	New Orleans	Santa Marta Cartagena Balboa Buenaventura Guayaquil Callao Matarani Antofagasta Valparaiso

AHOY!

Free baggage limit is 350 pounds. Lykes Lines will tell you the charges for excess baggage.
Pets, cars, and campers are accepted. Ask booking agent for rates.
Children's fares: 1 to 11 years—half fare; 12 and over—full fare.
Smallpox and cholera inoculations may be required. Ask agent.
Age limit: Passengers over 70 years are not accepted.

Fare	Duration of Trip	How Often Sails	Number of Passengers
$1530	41–51 days	every 12 days	12 or 8 (see entry)
$1650	45–55 days	every 12 days	12 or 8
$385	9 days	every 12 days	12 or 8
$385	3 days		
$385	6–11 days		
$385	15 days		
$490	10 days		
$630	12 days		
$700	17 days		
$735	20 days		
$770	22 days		

Lykes Lines
300 Poydras Street
New Orleans, Louisiana 70130
(504) 523-6611

Lykes Lines
Melrose Building
Houston, Texas 77002

Lykes Lines
320 California Street
San Francisco, California 94104

A Lykes Lines freighter *Lykes Lines*

Here's a review of some basic facts about Lykes. It has a fleet of forty-four ships of five classes: Pride, which carries eight passengers and has a lounge that doubles as a dining room between meal hours; Clipper, another passenger ship with a large lounge shared by passengers and ship's officers; Pacer, Andes, and "Roll-On, Roll-Off" vessels, all with separate passenger lounges, each of which carries twelve passengers per voyage. Staterooms on all ships are doubles with two bunks and a private bath. "Roll-On, Roll-Off" vessels spend shorter periods of time in port, generally between eight and twenty-four hours.

The food is American-style cuisine, and passengers and officers dine together.

Moore McCormack Lines

New York to east coast of South America ("The Brazilian Coffee Break" cruise); New York to selected ports on east coast ("The Gaucho" cruise); one-way trips to most ports

Moore McCormack, said to be the crème de la crème of freighters, describes the ambience on its South American cruise as that of an oceangoing house party—informal and relaxed, yet ebullient! Those who have taken this trip testify that the days speed by. Between ports, passengers prowl the ship, finding privacy if they desire or joining the others in the large passenger lounge to play darts, chat over their newspapers, or watch television—a special kick when you can pick up old American movies dubbed in Portugese. Of course, there's ample deck space, both open and enclosed, as well as a ship's store stocked with soft drinks, beer, wine, cigarettes, and the like.

Moore McCormack Lines

Moore McCormack Lines—South America

Type of Trip	From	To
"The Brazilian Coffee Break" cruise	New York	Rio de Janeiro Santos Bahia Recife Fortaleza
"The Gaucho" cruise	New York	Rio de Janeiro Santos Buenos Aires Montevideo
one way	New York	Rio de Janeiro or Santos
one way	New York	Montevideo or Buenos Aires

AHOY!

Free baggage limit is 20 cubic feet per full fare; 10 cubic feet per half fare.
Cars and pets not accepted.
Children's fares: under 12 years—half fare; over 12—full fare.
Age limits: No one under 5 years or over 79 years accepted due to lack of medical facilities. Persons over 65 years must submit a doctor's letter shortly before sailing verifying good health and the ability to make the voyage without a doctor in attendance.

A harbor scene, Rio de Janeiro   *Hammond Inc.*

Fare	Duration of Trip	How Often Sails	Number of Passengers
$2000 (double) $2300 (single) $150—surcharge, suite	30 days	3 to 4 times monthly	12
$2600 (double) $2300 (single) $150—surcharge, suite	40 days	3 to 4 times monthly	12
$950 (double) $1175 (single)	10–11 days	3 to 4 times monthly	12
$1300 (double) $1500 (single)	15 days	3 to 4 times monthly	12

Moore McCormack Lines Inc.
2 Broadway
New York, New York 10004
(212) 363-6600

A double room aboard a Moore McCormack freighter   *Moore McCormack Lines*

Each stateroom has air conditioning, wall-to-wall carpeting, and a private bath, not to mention such frills as mirrored walk-in closets, ample couches or chairs, and flowers and fruit courtesy of Moore McCormack. In addition to regular double or single staterooms, Moore McCormack offers three types of deluxe cabins in the Pride, Mariner, and Constellation classes (for a surcharge of $150 on "The Brazilian Coffee Break" cruise and $200 on "The Gaucho" cruise). So if you feel you want to splurge, consider reserving a deluxe cabin.

In the Pride class, there is one deluxe stateroom, Cabin 1, with two beds, two sofa beds, lounge chairs, and a private bath with both tub and shower, and it is close to the lounge, bar, and snack pantry. The Mariner category has two deluxe staterooms [Cabin 1 and Cabin 2] each with two beds, large bathrooms, and especially nice furniture. In Constellation class, Cabin 2 is the deluxe stateroom, a large room consisting of two sofa-type beds, an upper bed, two dressers, lounge chairs, a desk, and a private bath with tub and shower. It, too, abuts the lounge as well as the bar and pantry.

A few stipulations: Since no physician, nurse, or medical steward is aboard, the company will not accept passengers who, in the opinion of the cruise master, cannot safely make the voyage. Those usually deemed unacceptable—the list is rather long—are: people infirm by age, illness, or handicap (needing canes, crutches, and the like); individuals with a history of epilepsy, asthma, mental illness, contagious disease, heart disease, or other serious organic disorders; people who require such continuous medical attention as injections, dressings, or treatments; and, finally, expectant mothers five months or more into pregnancy. Women less than five months pregnant are accepted if their physician provides a certificate assuring that their pregnancy is normal and that they can comfortably and safely undertake such a trip.

By now you may be developing an immunity to the following warning, but we would be remiss not to remind you that Moore McCormack, like so many other freighter lines, cannot strictly adhere to its itinerary because the swift transport of cargo is its primary obligation. Your ship, therefore, having left from New York City, may not follow what would appear to be the most geographically logical route as it travels along the west coast of South America, that is, from northernmost to southernmost port. Instead, the ship might call first at Santos, Brazil, then head back to Recife in northeastern Brazil, then farther north to Fortaleza, the northernmost port, and only then south to Rio de Janeiro. So, be prepared to ramble around the west coast of South America for thirty or forty days, with perhaps merely a day's notice as to which port comes next.

Undoubtedly you've noticed from the chart that Moore McCormack offers one-way tickets to most of its ports. You should understand, however, that cruise passengers take precedence over one-way passengers, making one-way tickets somewhat ticklish to obtain. Even so, if you have the time, inclination, and patience to work out such passage with either the Moore McCormack booking agent or a travel agent, one-way travel is an excellent means of giving yourself latitude to range around South America. One recent Moore McCormack passenger went one way to Rio de Janeiro, stayed for nearly a *year* exploring the interior of Brazil, then simply registered himself on a wait list when he was ready to go home. Within a matter of weeks he hopped a ship back to New York. You may not have a year to spare, of course, but you get the idea.

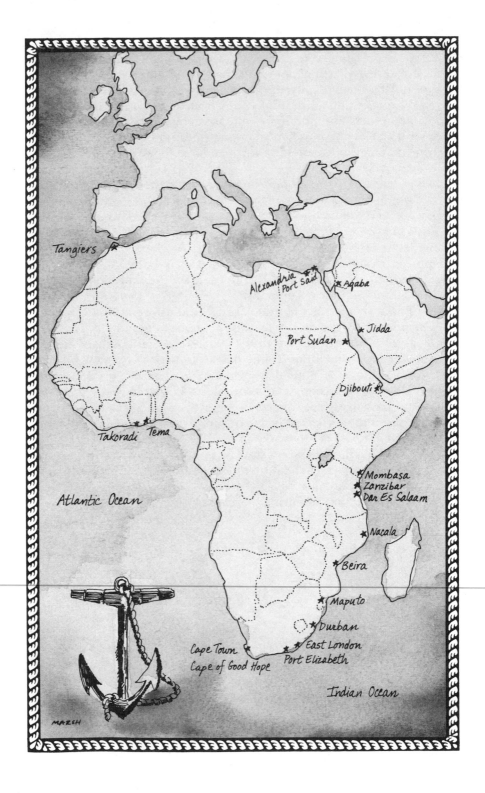

Tangiers ★

Alexandria ★ ★ Port Said ★ Aqaba

Port Sudan ★ ★ Jidda

Djibouti ★

Takoradi ★ ★ Tema

Atlantic Ocean

★ Mombasa
★ Zanzibar
★ Dar Es Salaam

★ Nacala

★ Beira

★ Maputo
★ Durban
★ East London
Cape Town ★ Port Elizabeth
Cape of Good Hope

Indian Ocean

MARCH

FIVE

AFRICA

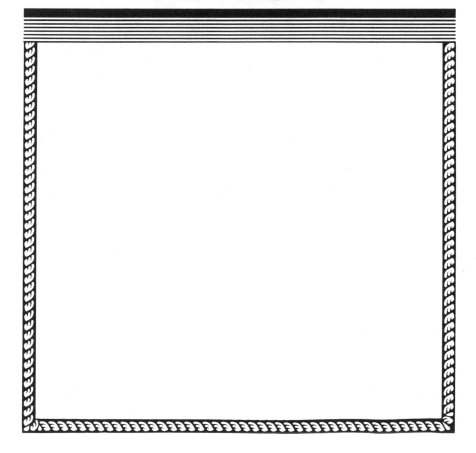

Advertisement for an African cruise, from the New York *Times*, June 10, 1956   *Farrell Lines*

Black Star Line

If you're game for an intriguing, slightly mysterious trip, consider shipping out with Black Star Line. Every two weeks a Black Star ship, carrying between ten and twelve passengers, leaves from either New York, Montreal, or Houston for West Africa.

Black Star's rules differ from those of most freighters. Passengers may not disembark until the ship reaches Ghana (Tema or Takoradi), even though the ship stops at a number of other ports along the coast of West Africa: Dakar, Freetown, Monrovia, Abidjan, Lagos, and Port Harcourt. When we inquired as to why the line restricted its passengers in this way, the Black Star staff demurred. One thing is certain, though, for a swift, interesting crossing to Ghana—one of Africa's most fascinating countries—Black Star can be relied upon.

Folks who have made the trip describe the line's ships as having modern, comfortable facilities. You can reserve either a double or single stateroom—some have private baths, others have shared bath—all the same price. There is ample deck space, both open and covered, as well as a large lounge with radio, television, books, games, and the like. Passengers are joined in the dining room and lounges by the ship's officers. Food on Black Star varies from standard continental fare to traditional African dishes.

Once you arrive in Ghana, which lies on the Gulf of Guinea, you'll almost certainly want to explore this historic country, the first in Africa to gain its independence. It has been a crucial trading state since 300 B.C., when Arab camel caravans trekked across the desert carrying salt, copper, and dried fruits from northern Africa. In 1471, Ghana was claimed by Portuguese explorers enthusiastic over its abundance of gold. What we now call Ghana was known as the Gold Coast until 1957, when it gained its independence from England and became the first member of the Commonwealth of Nations to be governed by black Africans.

Black Star Line—Africa

Type of Trip	From	To
one way	New York, Houston, or Montreal	Tema Takoradi

AHOY!

Free baggage limit is 40 cubic feet. Black Star will tell you the charges for excess baggage.

Passenger-accompanied cars are allowed; price is $128 per 40 cubic feet plus tax. No pets.

Children's fares: under 1 year—10% full fare; 1 to 3 years—25%; 3 to 12—50%; over 12—full fare.

Age limit: 65.

No women more than five months pregnant will be accepted for the voyage.

Fare	Duration of Trip	How Often Sails	Number of Passengers
$559.60	15 days	twice monthly	10 or 12

Black Star Line Ltd.
17 Battery Place, 5th Floor
New York, New York 10004
(212) 425-6100

Ghana is a vigorous commercial hub, and its splendid mineral and agricultural resources move out to the world from the ports where the Black Star ships call. Important exports are cacao (Ghana being the world's prime source), copra, coffee, kola nuts, palm oil, bauxite, manganese, gold, and timber.

Since Black Star prefers to sell one-way tickets, leaving the return voyage flexible, most travelers who make this trip take advantage of Ghana's geographical location to travel either northeast to Egypt, a relatively easy trip by either air or land, or northwest to Morocco, where you can easily cross (at the Strait of Gibraltar) into southern Spain. In fact, one can scarcely imagine a more convenient point than Ghana for touring Africa, not to speak of easy access to European countries such as Italy, Greece, Spain, and Portugal.

The life of leisure and the fresh salt air   *Cluett Peabody & Co. Inc.*

Hellenic Lines

New York, Houston, or New Orleans to east coast of Africa via Red Sea ports. May return to Savannah (Georgia)

Since Hellenic Lines was described in chapter 3, we will simply review the vital facts about accommodations at the end of this entry.

Hellenic's African cruise takes you from New York, Houston, or New Orleans over the Atlantic Ocean, across the equator, around the Cape of Good Hope, up the Indian Ocean into the Red Sea, and back down the east coast of Africa—truly a mind-boggling pilgrimage! You'll stop at Port Said, Egypt, on the Suez Canal; Aqaba, Jordan; Jidda, Saudi Arabia; Djibouti; Port Sudan, Sudan; Mombasa, Kenya; Tanga and Dar es Salaam, Tanzania; and Durban, South Africa.

Your first three stops take you through probably the most controversial and dynamic area in the world today. These ports will provide a glimpse not only into the past but into what will undoubtedly be the future of Egypt, Jordan, and Saudi Arabia—not to mention the countries whose development these three nations will affect.

As a passenger on a Greek (as opposed to an American) ship, you may well enjoy greater access to and freedom in the countries you visit. It should be stressed, however, that visas must be in order. Don't forget to contact either the visa service we suggested in chapter 2 as well as the consulates of each country, especially if you plan to take advantage of Hellenic's open-return ticket, which allows you to return any time within twelve months of your departure.

But let us brief you on some of the ports you'll visit. After leaving the Red Sea area, your Hellenic ship docks in Port Sudan, a vital seaport city of Sudan, the largest country in Africa. A north African land similar in many ways to Libya, Egypt, and Morocco in its culture, Sudan's diverse population includes Arabic-speaking Moslems, descendants of African Negroes, and Nubians, a dark-skinned people related to the early Egyptians and Ethiopians. Dating back to Biblical times, Sudan, with its historic

A banana carrier off the coast of Africa   *Leslie A. Wilcox, Blackey & Sons Publishers, London*

capital of Khartoum on the Nile River, presents enticing opportunities to strike out on an adventurous foray, maybe even to the Nubian Desert.

Sudan is a land of remarkable topographical and cultural variety. In the south, some of the world's tallest people live in a great swamp area surrounding the White Nile (a branch of the Nile) known as the equatorial region. In the steppe and savanna regions of central Sudan, nomads eke out a living from the parched land. The vast, largely unpopulated region in the north covers fully one-third of the country. At Khartoum (in central Sudan), the White Nile and the Blue Nile converge and flow to Egypt.

Major Sudanese exports are Egyptian cotton, hardwood, and gum arabic, which is used in making perfumes and candy. Sudan supplies nearly 90 percent of the world's peanuts, as well as large amounts of sesame seeds, coffee, and cassava.

From Port Sudan you move on to Djibouti, a fascinating city in the easternmost region of Africa, which stretches along the horn of Africa facing the Gulf of Aden on the north and the Indian Ocean on the east. Because of its location at the mouth of the Red Sea, the area around Djibouti formerly known as Somaliland has been overrun with Europeans since the mid-1800s. For numerous reasons, this may well be the most unusual stop on your Hellenic African cruise.

Hellenic Lines—Africa

Type of Trip	From	To
cruise	New York—may return to Savannah (Georgia)	Port Said Aqaba Jidda Port Sudan Djibouti Mombasa Tanga Dar es Salaam Durban
cruise	Houston or New Orleans—may return to Savannah	same ports

AHOY!

Free baggage limit is 25 cubic feet, 13 cubic feet for half fares. Ask Hellenic for excess baggage rates.

Cars can be taken on certain trips, as regular freight with a 25% discount. Pets are allowed with a vet's certificate and certificate of rabies inoculation: dogs $350; cats 200.

Children's fares: under 1 year—free; 1 to 12 years—half fare; over 12—full fare.

Smallpox and cholera inoculations are required. Check with Hellenic or consulates of countries to be visited for forther information.

Passengers 65 or over must submit a doctor's note stating that they are well enough to undertake the voyage.

Now for a quick recap on Hellenic Lines. The company's fleet consists of forty-two ships with excellent accommodations for twelve passengers per ship. A typical stateroom features two comfortable, full-size beds, several armchairs, a desk, dressing table, dresser, and private bathroom. The single stateroom is the same price, somewhat smaller, and its bed may be either a sofa bed or bunk. Other facilities on Hellenic ships include a dining room which serves Greek, continental, and American food; a lounge; a pantry for snacks; and open and enclosed deck areas, as on many ships.

If you are contemplating this trip and want to book as an open-return passenger, play it safe by contacting Hellenic Lines or a freighter travel agent well in advance.

Fare	Duration of Trip	How Often Sails	Number of Passengers
$4500	115–125 days	twice monthly	12
$4700	145 days	twice monthly	12

Hellenic Lines Ltd.
39 Broadway
New York, New York 10006
(212) 482-5694

Hellenic Lines
1314 Texas Avenue
Houston, Texas 77002
(713) 224-8607

Hellenic Lines
2812 International Trade Mart
New Orleans, Louisiana 70130
(504) 581-2825

Hellenic Lines
Filonos Street 61/65
Piraeus, Greece
417-1541

Deck life at the turn of the century
The Rubaiyat of Bridge, May Wilson Preston, Harpers © 1909

Moore McCormack Lines

New York to east coast of Africa via Cape of Good Hope ("African Odyssey" cruise) or additional ports ("Sea Safari" cruise), one-way trips to most ports

Accommodations on this fine freighter line were described in chapter 4, so we'll summarize the information at the end of this entry.

Moore McCormack's "African Odyssey" is certainly one of the most exciting of the freighter expeditions. Setting out from New York for six ports along the east coast of Africa, you sail across the Atlantic, passing over the equator, and then around the Cape of Good Hope—landmark for seafarers since the Vikings. Your first port of call is Cape Town, South Africa's oldest city, which is situated at the foot of Table Mountain. South Africa is the richest, most highly developed country in Africa, and examples of its modern technology are juxtaposed against its wild landscapes of high plateaus, towering mountains, deep valleys, and picturesque beaches along the fertile coast where tropical fruits thrive.

Along the area known as the Coastal Strip, you'll visit Port Elizabeth, East London, and Durban. This low-lying area, homeland of the Zulus, rises dramatically into magnificent mountains (the Drakenburg range). The chief exported crops from these ports include bananas, citrus fruits, sugarcane, and vegetables. Other exports are gold, diamonds, asbestos, chromite, coal, copper, iron ore, manganese, platinum, silver, and uranium. Many of South Africa's factories, producing chemicals, clothing, iron, steel, and other metals, are situated in the towns you visit. Cruising into these ports gives you a chance to see everything from Zulu huts on the plateaus to factories within the city limits.

As the cruise progresses, your ship docks at three coastal cities in Mozambique: Maputo, Beira, and Nacala. Also known as Portuguese East Africa, Mozambique plays a key role in the economies of its neighbors, South Africa, Malawi, Zambia, and Zimbabwe (formerly Rhodesia), providing manpower as well as access to the sea. More than 80 percent of the area's trade passes through the ports of Maputo and Beira.

AFRICA   81

Moore McCormack Lines—Africa

Type of Trip	From	To
"African Odyssey" cruise	New York	Cape Town Port Elizabeth East London Durban Maputo Beira Nacala
"Sea Safari" cruise	New York	Cape Town Port Elizabeth East London Durban Maputo Beira Nacala Dar es Salaam Mombasa
one way	New York	Cape Town Port Elizabeth East London Durban Maputo Beira Mombasa

AHOY!

Free baggage limit is 20 cubic feet per full fare, 10 cubic feet per half fare. Ask Moore McCormack for excess baggage rates.

Cars and pets are not accepted.

Children's fares: under 12 years—half fare; over 12—full fare.

Age limits: No one under 5 years or over 79 years accepted. Persons over 65 years must submit a doctor's letter shortly before sailing stating that their health is good and they can make the voyage without a doctor in attendance.

Fare	Duration of Trip	How Often Sails	Number of Passengers
$3300 (double) $3800 (single) $4000 (deluxe)	50 days	once every 3 weeks	12
$4000 (double) $4500 (single) $4800 (deluxe)	70 days	once every 3 weeks	12
$1150; 1400 $1250; 1500 $1350; 1600 $1450; 1700 $1600; 1850 $1700; 1950 $2000; 2250	(approx.) 16 days 18 days 20 days 22 days 24 days 26 days 35 days	once every 3 weeks	12

Moore McCormack Lines Inc.
2 Broadway
New York, New York 10004
(212) 363-6600

PRIDE CLASS
Displacement: 18,365 tons

CONSTELLATION CLASS
Displacement: 20,070 tons
27,898 tons⁰

MARINER CLASS
Displacement: 22,629 tons

Deck plans of three Moore McCormack classes, (from left) the Pride Class, the Constellation Class, and the Mariner Class *Moore McCormack Lines*

A mineral-rich country, Mozambique exports uranium, gold, silver, and other metals. Your ship, in fact, may either carry minerals, metals, or products like copra, sisal, cashew nuts, tea, or coconut palm. If there is time during your sojourn, consider a side trip to the island of Madagascar, 100 miles across the Mozambique Channel.

From Mozambique the African Odyssey cruise swings back to New York City, completing its circuit in a little over seven weeks.

The "Sea Safari" cruise hits basically the same ports but includes Dar es Salaam, Tanzania, and Mombasa, Kenya, up the coast from Nacala, Mozambique. If you can, plan to visit Zanzibar, the famous Isle of Cloves, just off Dar es Salaam, where you'll see traces of early Arabs and Persians in the area's architecture and handicrafts.

Tanzania would make an ideal one-way trip. In fact, many of the cruise members lament short port stops there. After all, the Serengeti Plain and Ngorongoro Crater boast the world's most spectacular game preserves, not to mention the surrounding countryside. Other unique sights close to Tanzanian ports include Kilimanjaro, Africa's highest mountain, which is located to the west of Mombasa, and Lake Victoria, Africa's largest lake. Tanzanian exports, some of which your ship will undoubtedly carry, are coffee, cotton, sisal, tea, cloves (from Zanzibar), tobacco, chili peppers, and millet, not to mention diamonds, of which thie country has one of the most important deposits in the world.

Back on the "Sea Safari," the last port of call on the east coast is Mombasa, Kenya, the second largest city in that independent republic. Tourists flock to Kenya at all times of the year to visit its wildlife parks and game preserves. Truly a fascinating country, Kenya is home to Arabs, Europeans, and Indians, as well as native Africans. Since Kenya warrants a lengthy stay, consider booking one-way passage to Mombasa. Transportation is excellent here too. For instance, you can take a leisurely train trip through the countryside where Masai tribesmen herd cattle over the plains against the backdrop of Nairobi National Park.

A special word to the travel wise: Moore McCormack's African cruises have been heavily booked recently. Be sure to plan well in advance of your desired departure date.

Full cruise passengers are booked first, so put in your bid for one-way booking six months or a year in advance. A freighter booking agent can be extremely helpful in obtaining a one-way passage though, be warned: successfully booking one way to Africa is tricky if not downright hard!

A Moore McCormack recap: The ships have handsomely furnished, spacious double and single staterooms, each with air conditioning, wall-to-wall carpeting, and private bath. Or you can reserve a deluxe stateroom for a surcharge of from $150 to $200. See chapter 4 for a description of the three types of deluxe staterooms.

A standard Moore McCormack stipulation: since the ships have no doctor aboard, the cruise master reserves the right to refuse passage to passengers considered physically unfit to make the trip. See chapter 4 for a list of those who are likely to be excluded for health reasons.

Moore McCormack Lines

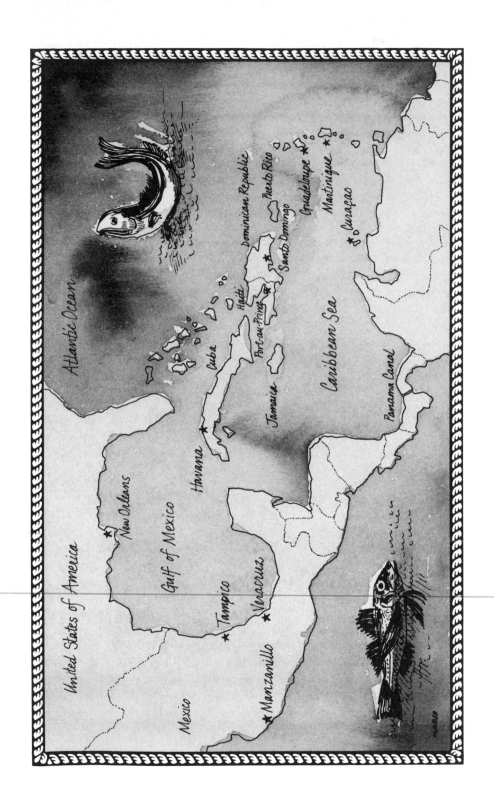

SIX

CARIBBEAN

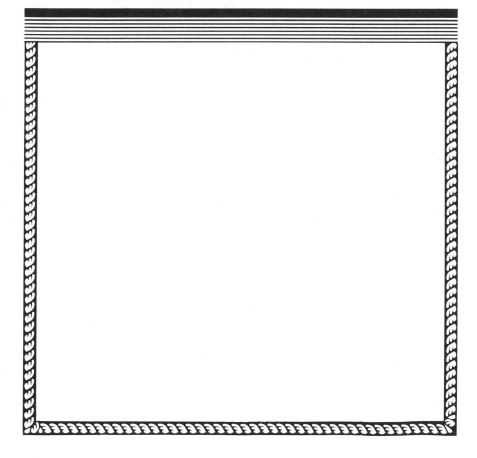

GREAT WHITE FLEET
Caribbean Cruises

GREAT WHITE FLEET

FOR more than a quarter of a century the Great White Fleet has been operating in the Caribbean. Its officers and men pioneered in the paths of Columbus, De Soto, Cabot, Drake and all the goodly company of adventurers that made Elizabethan days famous—and it is because of their experience that travel on ships of the Great White Fleet is made so luxurious for the Tourist of today. Spacious rooms—all outside—are necessary in the Tropics; so are wide decks on which to dance and play. And when you go adventuring in the Spanish Main you will appreciate the wonderful food and the fine personal service so characteristic of Great White Fleet Ships.

Sailings every week from NEW YORK and NEW ORLEANS on tours that last from nine to twenty-four days. Only first class passengers are carried and when you have bought your ticket there is no further expense; motor trips, hotel and railroad accommodations, launch trips are all included in the price you pay for your ticket. Plan your winter Vacation so as to include a Great White Fleet Tour through the Caribbean. You will enjoy a restful, interesting sea trip, managed by men who have made a study of conditions afloat and ashore in the Tropics.

Address Passenger Traffic Department

UNITED FRUIT COMPANY
17 Battery Place　　　Room 1631　　　New York City

Write for illustrated free booklets

Visit:	Jamaica	Panama Canal	Costa Rica	Colombia	Guatemala	British Honduras	Spanish Honduras
Cuba	Port Antonio	Zone	Port Limon	Cartagena	Puerto Barrios	Belize	Puerto Cortez
Havana	Kingston	Cristobal		Puerto Colombia	Guatemala City		Puerto Castilla
				Santa Marta			Tela

Advertisement in 1928 for Caribbean cruises　*United Fruit Co.*

Surinam Lines

New Orleans to the Caribbean via Paramaribo and certain Mexican Gulf ports; one-way trips to many of these ports

Surinam Lines, based in Surinam (formerly Dutch Guiana) but operating out of New Orleans, trades throughout the Caribbean on two vessels, the MV *Corantijn* and the MV *Saramacca*, each accommodating six passengers.

The MV *Corantijn*, built in 1968, has three double cabins and one single, all with lower and upper berths and private baths, as does its sister ship, the MV *Saramacca*. Accommodations on Surinam Lines aren't exactly swank but certainly suffice.

As with most freighters, the exact itinerary remains open until several days before departure. As you know by now, flexibility and freighter travel go hand-in-hand. Surinam Lines, being principally a cargo service, must at all times fit its schedule to the demands of its employers, and thus schedules develop as need dictates. Sometimes ports are added to its original itinerary; sometimes ports are deleted. Remember, though, a port skipped on the southbound trip may well be called on the northbound trip. Within two weeks of your sailing date, your Surinam Line booking agent should finalize your itinerary. It's a good idea to call and inquire.

All Surinam Line ships invariably call at their home port of Paramaribo, Surinam, remaining there at least four days to two weeks. Because the crew is off duty there, you'll have a chance to stay in the city, instead of staying on the ship as is customary. Don't fret about getting a hotel ashore; As part of the cruise package, the passenger agent will make a reservation for you at a Paramaribo hotel.

Other frequent ports of call include various islands in the West Indies: Martinique, Guadeloupe, Aruba, Curacao, and Santa Domingo, all well-known resorts that would cost far more to visit were you traveling on a conventional Caribbean cruise line. Most likely you'll stay in these ports for only a few days, long enough to savor the island if it's your first visit or to revive old memories if you've stopped there before.

Surinam Lines—Caribbean

Type of Trip	From	To
cruise	New Orleans	Paramaribo Martinique, Guadeloupe Aruba Curaçao Santo Domingo Haiti New Orleans Tampico Veracruz Belém
one way	New Orleans	Paramaribo Martinique, Guadeloupe Haiti Tampico or Veracruz

AHOY!

The baggage limit on Surinam Lines is 100 pounds. Ask Surinam Lines for excess rate.
Cars can be taken along at the prevailing freight rate. No pets allowed.
Children's fares: under 12—half fare.
Surinam Lines will accept no passengers over the age of 55, since the ships have no doctor or nurse.

Port-au-Prince, Haiti, another frequent Surinam Lines port, never fails to please visitors with its amazing, diverse tropical pleasures, entertainment, cuisine, landmarks, and beaches.

But those who have traveled this route with Surinam seem most impressed by two lesser-known ports on the east coast of Mexico—Veracruz and Tampico. Both of these quaint seaports amaze tourists whose interest in Mexico has been dulled by either rumor or a firsthand experience of commercialized resorts like Acapulco and Mazatlan. In the earthy, congenial towns of Veracruz and Tampico, the indigenous culture flourishes amidst just enough modernity to meet your needs. Truly a different aspect of Mexico!

Another Surinam Lines Caribbean port, Belém, located on the northeast coast of Brazil at the mouth of the Amazon River, plays a key role in that country's economy. Most of Brazil's invaluable products—coffee, cacao beans, sugarcane, soybeans, iron ore, and a wide range of minerals—

Fare	Duration of Trip	How Often Sails	Number of Passengers
$750	4–5 weeks	twice monthly	6
$400	2 weeks	twice monthly	6
$350	10 days	twice monthly	
$250	4–5 days	twice monthly	
$150	2–3 days	twice monthly	

Hansen & Tideman Inc.
442 Canal Street
New Orleans, Louisiana 70130
(504) 586-8755

are brought up the river to meet trade ships docked in Belém. In addition, the city provides enticing, sensual Caribbean diversions, though it is a vital port rather than a tourist trap.

Considering incredibly thrifty fares and the unique cities you visit, Surinam Lines to the Caribbean is a vacationing must.

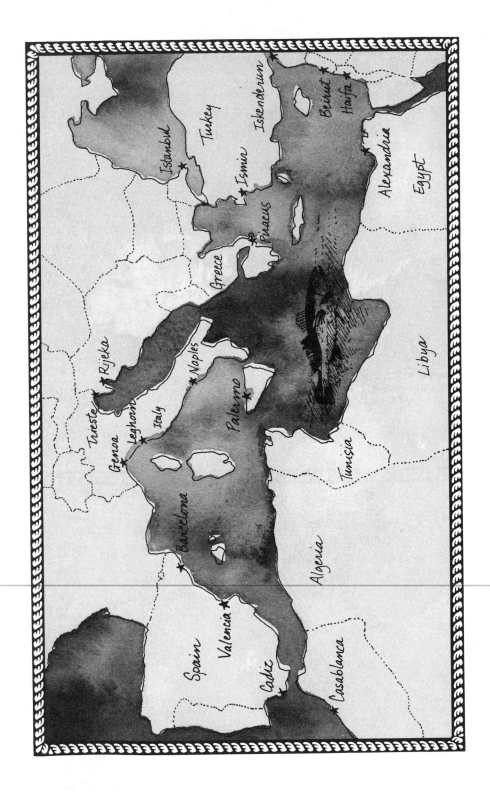

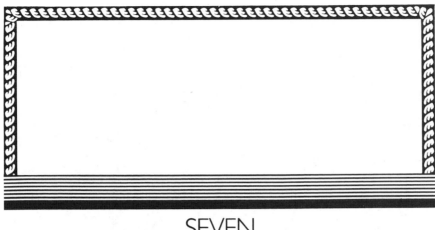

SEVEN

MEDITERRANEAN

RESERVED...a gondola for two

WHETHER you glide along the Grand Canal under the witchery of a Venetian moon or visit other glamorous places . . . in Italy, Spain, France, Greece, Egypt, the Holy Land . . . nowhere else will you find such sheer adventure and delight as in the lands bordering the Mediterranean.

Here, American Export will bring to American travelers, in the not too distant future, the rich experience of a Mediterranean cruise—with a fleet of modern passenger liners designed to exacting American standards of comfort and pleasure.

Here, too, American Export will continue to foster the best traditions of our American Merchant Marine with fast, dependable cargo liners operated on schedules keyed to American needs.

AMERICAN EXPORT LINES

25 Broadway, New York 4, N. Y.

| MEDITERRANEAN | BLACK SEA | RED SEA | INDIA | CEYLON | BURMA |

TIME, FEBRUARY 2, 1948

Not all time on a freighter cruise is spent on the high seas. *American Export Lines*

Farrell Line

New York to Egypt via Palermo

Farrell, an old, reliable, and popular freighter line, provides excellent passenger accommodations to the Mediterranean via Egypt, as well as Australia (discussed in chapter 9). On the eastbound Mediterranean voyage, Farrell ships carry manufactured goods—clothing, refrigerators, cameras—and return with such imports as tobacco, wine, and olive oil. Farrell ships have six larger-than-average staterooms, which are air conditioned, situated outside, and equipped with private bathrooms. The cabins also feature double berths; if you're traveling alone, you pay double or take on a roommate.

Farrell's Mediterranean cruise, thrifty beyond belief, touches some of the world's most glorious cities. After cruising from New York across the Atlantic through the Strait of Gibraltar and along the northern coast of Africa, you enter the Mediterranean heading for Palermo, Sicily. From there you sail to Piraeus, near Athens, then around the horn of Greece into the Aegean Sea, up to Istanbul on the Sea of Marmara.

After Istanbul, the ship again enters the Aegean Sea, pulls into its second Turkish port, Izmir, then skirts the coast of Turkey past the island of Cyprus to Iskenderun, Turkey. From there you cross the Aegean Sea to the continent of Africa, docking in Alexandria, Egypt. Usually there is a second westbound stop at Palermo before cruising out the Mediterranean to Cádiz at the southernmost tip of Spain, and then you head across the Atlantic and home.

It was on Farrell's Mediterranean voyage that Clara Wallach discovered the fascination of cargo operations. By talking to crew members, she learned that a freighter's workhorse duties are far from a simple matter of

Farrell Line—Mediterranean

Type of Trip	From	To
cruise	New York	Palermo
		Piraeus
		Istanbul
		Izmir
		Iskenderun
		Alexandria
		Palermo
		Cádiz

AHOY!

Free baggage limit is 300 pounds. Ask Farrell for excess baggage rates.
Cars can be taken; pets are not allowed.
Children's fares: under 12 years—half fare.
Passengers over 75 years are not eligible. Those over 65 must provide a Farrell Line medical certificate signed by both passenger and doctor. Also, no children under 18 months of age.

The *African Enterprise* and the *African Moon* working offshore cargo at the Farrell Lines terminal in Brooklyn, New York   *Farrell Line*

Fare	Duration of Trip	How Often Sails	Number of Passengers
$2800	35–40 days	every 2 weeks	12

Farrell Line
1 Whitehall Street
New York, New York 10004
(212) 440-4227 Cable FARSHIP

hoisting crates from ship to shore. After each port stop, the remaining cargo must be redistributed, lest the shift of ballast affect the ship's stability. "I know this sounds odd," Clara says, "but I used to sit on deck watching the crew unload while everyone else was on shore touring!"

Her husband, Jesse, who has traveled extensively for fifty-five years, looks back on the moment when he and Clara sailed into Istanbul harbor on this trip as the most thrilling single experience of all his global peregrinations. "The night before," he recalls, "we anchored outside the harbor. About 5 A.M. we were awakened by tugs coming alongside to tow us in. My first reaction when I got up and looked out the porthole was disappointment—the city was shrouded in heavy mist, and I'd been waiting years to see the skyline from the harbor. But suddenly as we approached, the mist cleared and I saw the six gold spires of the Blue Mosque! Breathtaking sight!"

As "freighter freaks," Jesse and Clara Wallach, who have made three major freighter voyages in the last four years, gladly cope with minimal frills. Thus, Jesse and Clara came equipped with everything from ice cubes and champagne to watercress sandwiches when they and a few friends came down to the dock to celebrate their departure for the Mediterranean. But just as they were about to pop the cork on a bottle of champagne, the first mate knocked on their door to announce a bon voyage party on the house. As we've said, freighter travel abounds with surprises!

The Wallachs mention a further delight on this trip—the dashing, avuncular first mate who joined them for dinner each evening. Clara still marvels at his endless store of entertaining anecdotes and monologues.

Hellenic Lines

New York to Beirut via Piraeus and Salonika; New Orleans or Houston to same ports; one-way trips to same ports

We've discussed Hellenic Lines in chapters 3 and 5, but should you have skipped those trips, there's a brief rundown on Hellenic vital facts at the end of this entry.

Mediterranean cruises are among the most sought-after, and Hellenic's are particularly popular, since the remarkable city of Piraeus is the line's home port.

Before we go any farther, though, let's consider a special feature of Hellenic's Mediterranean service—the open-return ticket, which allows you to stay in either Piraeus, Salonika, or Beirut for up to twelve months before cruising home. This is an offer unique among freighter companies. Without even committing yourself to an approximate return date, you simply purchase an eastbound ticket. When you decide on your return date, you just contact the closest Hellenic agent and reserve a stateroom for the westbound voyage. Caution: be sure at the outset that your ticket agent or travel agent understands that you want an open-return ticket.

Now the itinerary. Piraeus, a gold coin's throw from Athens, will undoubtedly overwhelm you. "Greek freaks," that grand fraternity of travelers who return again and again to Greece, consider Piraeus the ideal starting point for your stay, be it a brief port stop or an extended tour. Even with two days in port, there's time to see downtown Athens, hike up to the Acropolis, see the Temple of Zeus, and visit countless other monuments. If, that is, you can extricate yourself from the sidewalk cafes where garrulous Greek waiters ply you with ouzo, a colorless, anise-flavored Greek liqueur, or that gritty Greek coffee, which the natives swill by the gallon, or delectable Greek pastries. As you'll see for yourself, Greeks live as if every day were their last and tend to consider it their mission to seduce visitors with every hedonistic enticement their bountiful Mediterranean souls can muster.

For a short tour of Piraeus, buses are cheap and quite manageable—

Hellenic Lines—Mediterranean

Type of Trip	From	To
cruise	New York	Piraeus Salonika Beirut
cruise	New Orleans or Houston	Piraeus Salonika Beirut
one way	New York	Piraeus
one way	New York	Salonika
one way	New York	Beirut

AHOY!

Free baggage limit is 25 cubic feet for full fares; 13 cubic feet for half fares. Ask Hellenic for excess baggage rates.

Cars can be taken on certain trips as regular freight with 25% discount. Pets are permitted with vet's certificate and rabies inoculation certificate at $350 for dogs, $200 for cats.

Children's fares: under 1 year—free; 1 to 12 years—half fare; over 12 years—full fare.

Passengers 65 years or over must submit doctor's certificate of good health.

Fare	Duration of Trip	How Often Sails	Number of Passengers
$1800 (double) $2000 (single)	50–60 days	twice monthly	12
$2500 (double) $2800 (single)	65–75 days	twice monthly	12
$475 (double) $550 (single)	18 days	twice monthly	12
$527 (double) $575 (single)	22 days	twice monthly	12
$700 (double) $750 (single)	26 days	twice monthly	12

Hellenic Lines
39 Broadway
New York, New York 10006
(212) 482-5694

Hellenic Lines
1314 Texas Avenue
Houston, Texas 77002
(713) 224-8607

Hellenic Lines
2812 International Trade Mart
New Orleans, Louisiana 70130
(504) 581-2825

Hellenic Lines
Filonos Street 61/65
Piraeus, Greece
417-1541

again, thanks to helpful Greeks. The trolley around the yacht harbor is popular, as is the twelve-hour trip to Delphi, with castles and ruins all along the way. Another possibility is the ferry to nearby Crete, Rhodes, or both!

Your second stop, Salonika, on the Aegean Sea, also offers many sightseeing opportunities. In fact, the majority of travelers advise taking an open-return ticket to Greece. "You just can't see enough on the cruise," they chorus.

Beirut, Lebanon, the final stop on Hellenic's Mediterranean cruise, was settled in 2000 B.C. as a Phoenician seaport and is known as the gateway between Asia and Europe. You'll find it vastly different from Piraeus, although equally rich in monuments—Phoenician, Roman, and Christian. It is a distinctly Arab country, although many people speak French and English as well as Arabic. Almost every sort of Lebanese makes his or her way to Beirut, so you're guaranteed a crash course in Lebanese culture. Poor traders from the mountains come to town dressed in colorful tunics, sheiks in red fezzes stroll around the boulevards European style, admiring fashion-conscious women decked out in high style. Don't fail to sample Lebanese foods—yogurt (not like your quick-lunch type, either, but rich and sweeter), flat bread, bulgur (cracked wheat), and of course lamb, that ubiquitous Mediterranean specialty.

Now your Hellenic capsule briefing. The company's fleet consists of forty-two ships with excellent accommodations for twelve passengers per ship. A typical double stateroom features two comfortable beds, several armchairs, a desk, dressing table, dressers, and a private bathroom. The single is the same price, and except for the bed, either a sofa bed or a bunk, is otherwise the same. Other facilities include a big dining room, lounge, pantry for snacks, and open and enclosed deck areas. Continually singled out for perhaps the finest food on any freighter line, Hellenic's chefs serve excellent Greek food as well as French, Italian, and even a few American specialties.

A word of warning: Hellenic agents stress, modestly of course, that their trips get more popular each year. It is best to plan early and contact a travel agent as soon as possible to make your reservations. (Even a year isn't too soon.)

Greek fishing vessels at berth   *Antoine Bon and Fernand Chapoutier*

Jugolinija Line

New York or Norfolk to Yugoslavia via Casablanca, Valencia, and other Mediterranean ports; one-way trips to numerous Mediterranean ports

Yugolinija, the Yugoslavian line, offers a wide variety of trips, both cruises and one way, to numerous enticing ports in the Mediterranean, as you can see from the accompanying chart. The major cruise, ending in Rijeka, Yugoslavia, has become increasingly popular as word has spread about the beauty of the Yugoslavian coast—from Rijeka, the northernmost coastal city, to Dubrovnik near the Albanian border.

A special feature of Jugolinija, an extremely helpful company when it comes to booking, are its arrangements with several major airlines to fly either way. Often, travelers want to cross by freighter but haven't enough time to return by sea. Here's the solution. As you might imagine, the rates for such specially planned trips are far more reasonable than they would be if made through an independent agent. Consider this option before you book passage, though, since changing tickets may be impossible.

Several special stipulations apply to Jugolinija. First, accommodations differ depending on whether you book the full cruise or one way. On the cruise, you may choose from three classes: first, cabin, and tourist. First and cabin classes both have two berths with a sofa bed and private bath. In cabin class the staterooms are also somewhat smaller. In tourist class you have no private bath; passengers share a total of four communal baths.

Those who have shipped out with Jugolinija find the staterooms quite comfortable; all have an outside porthole, carpeting, a dressing table area, and a sitting area with sofa, coffee table, and armchairs. Both first class and cabin class staterooms are situated on the first class deck, which has an outdoor verandah and bar at one end and the first class dining room at the other. One deck below are the tourist class cabins and dining room.

For one-way trips, you can travel in either a Class A or a Class T stateroom. Class A is a two-berth cabin with bath; Class T is a two-berth cabin with bath outside, which you may or may not share with other passengers.

One further detail: Jugolinija's rates change depending on when you travel. On-season, April 16 to September 15, rates are 10 percent more than those during the line's off-season, September 16 through April 16.

The facilities on all Jugolinija sister ships include: open shelterdeck with forecastle and poop deck, an ideal place for strolling and mingling with fellow passengers; the lounges, equipped with radio, stereo, reading material, and games; the bar, snack pantry, and dining room. Food on Jugolinija is ample and tasty, since its cooks have mastered both native eastern European and international cuisine. One passenger told of a Chinese chef several years ago who turned out everything from apple strudel to wonton soup. Also, bars on Jugolinija's ships are well stocked with fine wines as well as hard liquor.

A few veterans of Jugolinija trips have come back somewhat disgruntled. In the interest of keeping you fully informed, we thought it worth reporting the following common complaints: crew members invading deck areas reserved for passengers, no laundry service, no fresh fruit or vegetables, non-English-speaking officers, lack of communication between staff and passengers about position, chart, mileage, and the like.

Naturally, many freighter freaks cheerfully accept such inconveniences, especially since Jugolinija offers the thriftiest Mediterranean cruises.

On the positive side, Jugolinija fans counter with raves for the spectacular Yugoslav coastline with its charm-filled cities beside the glistening Adriatic where one is spoiled by hospitable restaurateurs serving up feasts of barbecued veal and seafood, not to mention that notoriously potent drink called slibovitz.

A 7,500 ton freighter of the Jugolinija Line   *Jugolinija Line*

Jugolinija Line—Mediterranean

Type of Trip	From	To
cruise	New York or Norfolk (Virginia)	Casablanca Tangier Valencia Genoa Naples Trieste Rijeka
one way	New York	Morocco or Lisbon
one way	New York	Various ports in Spain, Savona, Genoa, Leghorn, Naples
one way	New York	Venice, Trieste, Rijeka

AHOY!

Free baggage limit is 100 kilos. Ask Jugolinija for excess baggage rates.
Cars can be carried at $140 for up to 1000 kilos, $300 for over 1000 kilos; pets are not allowed.
Children's fares: Under 2 years—free; 2 to 12 years—half fare; over 12 years—full fare. Additional children of any age—quarter fare.
Age limit: 75 years of age.

(On-season rates; for off-season, 9/16 to 4/15, deduct 10%)

▼

Fare	Duration of Trip	How Often Sails	Number of Passengers
$2200 (first class) $2200 (cabin) $1800 (tourist)	40–50 days	every 10 days	12
$500 (Class A*) $350 (Class T*)	8–10 days	every 10 days	12
$800 (Class A*) $600 (Class T*)	12 days	every 10 days	12
$1000 (Class A*) $800 (Class T*)	21–25 days	every 10 days	12

*See text for an explanation of Class A and T.

Jugolinija-Yugoslav Line
N.E.W.S. Shipping Co.
19 Rector St.—36th Floor
New York, New York 10016
(212) 248-4500

Lykes Lines

New Orleans or Tampa to Haifa via Casablanca and Barcelona; one-way trips to most Mediterranean ports

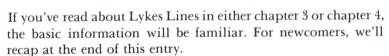

If you've read about Lykes Lines in either chapter 3 or chapter 4, the basic information will be familiar. For newcomers, we'll recap at the end of this entry.

Many have taken the Lykes Mediterranean cruise and agree that one can scarcely have anything but a memorable escapade given dependable service by the ship's efficient staff and the incomparable ports. The report of Donna Claren tells the story.

★ ★

Donna, a retired insurance agent from Houston, Texas, came home transformed from the Lykes Mediterranean cruise, her first sea venture. The crossing pleased her— "seemed so quick!"—particularly after the ship hit the Gulf Stream and experienced ten perfect days in open ocean. But landing in Casablanca, Donna says, was unforgettable.

It was a land of seemingly wary, odd Arabs hiding under the hoods of their djellabas, peering out to offer a tourist anything from an orange to a "diamond" bracelet, all the while chanting, "Only twenty dirams, Missie, twenty dirams only for English." During Donna's stop in Casablanca there was time enough for a bus trip to Rabat, the new capital of Morocco and, in contrast to Casablanca, a far more sophisticated, modern city. But when she returned to Casablanca, with one remaining day before moving on to Barcelona, Donna couldn't resist the insistent guides who thronged around the passengers wherever they went, and she persuaded some of her fellow passengers to

The *Joseph Lykes*   *Lykes Lines*

venture on a tour of the Casbah. Descending deep into the dark, labyrinthine bazaar where Moroccans hawk their wares amidst crowds of heavily laden donkeys, old men bound for the mosque, and tourists from every conceivable nation, Donna for the first time felt the full excitement of the voyage she had undertaken. "Casablanca set the tone for my whole vacation. Actually I began to worry that the rest would be anti-climatic, but then Alexandria and Istanbul knocked me out too!"

Donna, scheduled to be back in Houston for a wedding, regretted her time restrictions. (Several one-way passengers on the cruise disembarked at Genoa or Piraeus.) She came home vowing to take the trip again with a few friends, hop off at Casablanca, and really see all of Morocco—and by the time you read this, she probably has done it, too!

Lykes Lines—Mediterranean

Type of Trip	From	To
cruise	New Orleans or Tampa	Assorted Mediterranean ports
cruise	Great Lakes ports	Mediterranean and Black Sea ports
one way	New Orleans or Tampa	Casablanca Barcelona Genoa Piraeus Istanbul, Izmir Iskenderun Beirut Alexandria Haifa

AHOY!

Free baggage limit is 350 pounds. Ask Lykes Lines for excess baggage charges.
Pets, cars, and campers are accepted. Ask booking agent for rates.
Children's fares: 1 to 11 years—half fare; 12 and over—full fare.
Age limit: Passengers over 70 years are not accepted.

Here's a quick recap about Lykes. There are five types of ships: Pride, which carries eight passengers and has a lounge that doubles as a dining room between meal hours; Clipper, an eight-passenger ship with a large lounge shared by passengers and ship officers; Pacer, Andes, and "Roll-On, Roll-Off" vessels, all with separate passenger lounges, carrying twelve passengers each. Staterooms on all Lykes ships are double with two bunks and a private bath. "Roll-On, Roll-Off" vessels spend shorter periods of time in port, generally between eight and twenty-four hours. On all ships, passengers and officers dine together on American-style food.

Fare	Duration of Trip	How Often Sails	Number of Passengers
$2100	60–70 days	every 2 weeks	8 or 12
$2625	65–75 days	every 2 weeks	8 or 12
$490 $625 $735 $630; 1050 $630; 1050 $6655; 1155 $6655; 1155 $6655; 1155 $6655; 1155		every 2 weeks	8 or 12

Lykes Lines
300 Poydras Street
New Orleans, Louisiana 70130
(504) 523-6611

Lykes Lines
Melrose Building
Houston, Texas 77002

Lykes Lines
320 California Street
San Francisco, California 94104

Prudential Lines

New York, Baltimore, Norfolk, or Charleston to Cádiz, Port Said, Istanbul, and other Mediterranean ports

Gather more than four freighter buffs together and Prudential Lines is likely to come up in their conversation within minutes! As you will soon appreciate, Prudential presents the ultimate chance for economical ocean vagabonding.

Three Prudential ships offer passenger accommodations—the LASH *Atlantico*, LASH *Pacifico*, and LASH *Italia*, each with four outside staterooms designed for two adults apiece. Much could be said in praise of Prudential's staterooms, but we'll just mention the unique extras—individually controlled air conditioning, your own refrigerator, telephones in each room for intership communication (if necessary, ship-to-shore calls can be made via communications satellite).

As for other facilities onboard: Movies are shown twice weekly in the passenger lounge, where card games and other entertainment go on continually, and a well-stocked library provides novels, magazines from the four continents, and even newspapers. By far the ship's most popular hangout is the deck, where Prudential's attentive stewards supply deck chairs and lap robes to help passengers take full advantage of the unique fun of a sea voyage—watching for whales, tracking bird flocks, or simply snoozing in the sun.

Prudential calls its Mediterranean cruise a "personal sea odyssey." If you go, you'll be one of only eight passengers spending thirty-two days at sea, crossing the Atlantic Ocean and the Mediterranean, visiting seven countries. The ship sails from New York, then puts in at Baltimore, Norfolk, and Charleston before crossing the Atlantic to Cádiz, Spain. You continue on through the Strait of Gibraltar (and the famed Rock) into the Mediterranean, with stops at Naples and Genoa, Italy. For many, the high point of the cruise is the stop in Alexandria, Egypt, where there will be ample time to visit Cairo, the Pyramids, and other spectacular sights in the area. From there it's on to Haifa, then up the Aegean Sea through the

A freighter of the Prudential Lines *Prudential Lines*

Prudential Lines—Mediterranean

Type of Trip	From	To
cruise	New York, Baltimore, Norfolk, or Charleston	Cádiz Naples Alexandria Port Said Haifa Istanbul Constanţa Genoa

AHOY!

Free baggage limit is 500 pounds, excess at $.03 per pound.
Cars are not carried, nor can pets be taken along.
Children's fares: up to 12 years—half fare.
Passengers 65 to 75 years must present doctor's certificate of good health.
    Over 76 cannot be accepted.

Bosporus to the Black Sea and Costanţa, Romania (with perhaps a side-trip to Bucharest aboard a Danube steamship), then back to Istanbul, Turkey. These are Prudential's definite ports; however, you may well find yourself calling at a number of other Middle Eastern cities too.

Graduates (as they call themselves) of this tour seem to be most impressed with Cádiz, perhaps because it's the first port after the crossing. In any event, it's an utterly charming city—home port of Columbus, whose statue you see staring at you when you dock—with a downtown section of exquisite tiny squares where the Spaniards cavort until all hours. Americans are always surprised to learn that the established dinner hour is 9 or 10 P.M., after which residents of Cádiz migrate into the center of town to stroll down modern promenades built between the looming, delicately-lit houses and huge but tasteful department stores.

Another often-discussed stop on this route, Istanbul, draws mixed reactions. Some abhor its noisy, crowded streets where travelers are apt to be hounded by "helpful" young boys or insistent merchants. A trustworthy guide helps a lot here, which Prudential personnel will gladly arrange. Hiring a cab for several people works well, if you can find a driver who won't fleece you. Outwitting the Turks strikes some visitors as challenging; others recoil and, in fact, remain piqued long after they are safely home

Fare	Duration of Trip	How Often Sails	Number of Passengers
$3150	42 days	weekly	8

(Approximate for one-way trips)

Prudential Lines Inc.
One World Trade Center
New York, New York 10048
(212) 775-0550 or 800-221-4118

because of one smarmy cab driver who charged outrageous fares. Nonetheless, everyone unanimously agrees you must take a boat trip up the Bosporus. (With the new bridge over the Bosporus, the view from a boat is even more impressive.)

After a recent trip, comments frequently heard about the stop in Alexandria were mainly compliments for the purser, who arranged sightseeing tours skillfully and cheerfully. Of course, everyone who visits these countries is desperate to see and do everything, as the Prudential staff understands. If you wish, they'll even have a camel and driver awaiting you at the dock!

Sweden

★ Göteborg

North Sea

★ Liverpool

London

★ Southampton

★ Rotterdam

★ Antwerp

★ Le Havre

France

★ Hamburg
Bremenhaven

★ Gdynia

Poland

EIGHT

NORTHERN EUROPE

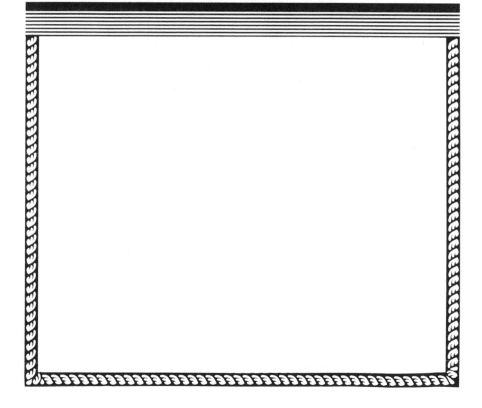

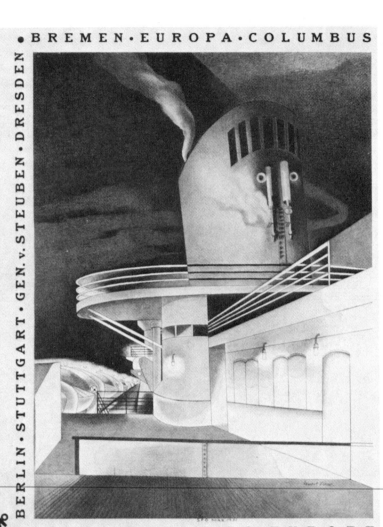

A 1931 advertisement for the Lloyd Line   *Estate of Ernest Fiene, courtesy of ACA Galleries*

Compagnie Generale Maritime

Port Elizabeth (New Jersey), Oakland, San Francisco, and Vancouver to Le Havre, possibly via Southampton or Antwerp. West Coast trips return to Long Beach (California).

 If you're in the market for a swift, bargain-priced, and decidedly pleasant means of reaching France, Compagnie Generale Maritime is definitely for you. No matter where you live, these French freighters leave from enough ports on both coasts to make reaching the boat a simple matter: Port Elizabeth, New Jersey (part of the Port of New York and within a ten-minute taxi ride of Manhattan); Oakland, San Francisco, and even sometimes Vancouver, British Columbia. (And, should you get the yen for a cruise down the Pacific Coast, you can hit all three West Coast ports before crossing the ocean.)

Everybody adores the French touch—in food, clothing, architecture—and the Compagnie Generale Maritime affords that distinctive Gallic mixture of beauty and excellence. Its impeccable container ships carry very few passengers—only a lucky two or five are selected for each voyage—housed in one double cabin or three singles, all with private baths. Not surprisingly, the dining room has a stylish, *intimé* charm—passengers share three tables with the captain and first mate. Rumor has it that the cuisine rates up to three stars: puffy croissants and café au lait in the morning, served with French sweet butter; country sausages and pâtés or cheeses at lunch (along with excellent wines); and fabulous dinner entrées with pastries, cheeses, and brandy.

But take a hint. Compagnie Generale Maritime's ships are difficult to book, and there's always a waiting list. If you want to join its elite group of passengers, contact a travel or freighter agent as soon as you possibly can.

If you lack resolve, just picture this: One warm night, after a delicious supper, you're on deck watching the lights of a passing ship twinkle in the distance, the scent of a French sailor's Gauloise drifting by on the wind! Eight days later (if you embarked from the East Coast, of course) you're in France! Need we say more?

Compagnie Generale Maritime—Northern Europe

Type of Trip	From	To
one way	Port Elizabeth (New Jersey)	Le Havre, possibly via Southampton and Antwerp
one way	Oakland, returning to Long Beach (California)	Le Havre, possibly via Southampton and Antwerp
one way	San Francisco	same
one way	Vancouver	same

AHOY!

Free baggage limit is 150 kilos per passenger. Ask C.G.M. for excess baggage rate.

Cars are not permitted. Pets may accompany owners. Ask C.G.M. for charges.

Children's fares: ages 5 to 12—30%; over 12—full fare.

No passengers over 75 or under 5 years are accepted. People over 65 must sign a release absolving C.G.M. of any medical responsibility, as well as a doctor's letter attesting to the passenger's ability to make the voyage without significant health problems.

Fare	Duration of Trip	How Often Sails	Number of Passengers
$750	8 days	every 3 weeks	2–5
$1270	25 days	every 2 months	2
$1320	26 days	every 2 months	2
$2900	56 days	every 2 months	2

Compagnie Generale Maritime
25 Broadway, Suite 1006
New York, New York 10004
(212) 425-5443

C.G.M.
Kerr Steamship Co. Inc.
1 Market Plaza, Suite 2400
Spear Tower
San Francisco, California 94105

Gdynia Line

Port Newark (New Jersey), New York, Baltimore, Wilmington, and some North Carolina ports to Rotterdam and Antwerp; Bremerhaven and Hamburg; and Gdynia. Return to New York City only.

 Freighter buffs who have made frequent crossings to northern Europe speak affectionately of Gdynia, the Polish-American line. Apparently a certain esprit makes for happy traveling with impromptu parties "on the house," all-night poker games, musical performances by members of the crew, and general merriment.

One lady, felled by *mal de mer* toward the end of the trip, told of a concerned steward's ministrations—hourly doses of strong broth, tea, and a hot toddy at cocktail time. Further comfort, she relates, came from knowing that her car was on board too. "What could be more practical than speeding away from the dock in my own little Peugeot, bound for Bruges," she commented.

Facilities aboard Gdynia Line are as cozy as the extras are welcome. Several passengers pointed out that staterooms on Gdynia are far larger than those on passenger-only ships. There are five double cabins and two single cabins, both types with private baths. The same fares apply to double and single cabins, though a 10 percent surcharge is added for the use of a single cabin. By the same token, should only one person occupy a double cabin, the fare is half again the regular fare. As you probably noticed on the chart, two fares apply. The first is for off-season—October 1 to May 31— the second for on-season, June 1 to September 30.

Besides the staterooms, Gdynia ships have two or three sitting rooms, a fine large dining room, and several deck areas.

All Gdynia ships start at Port Newark, New Jersey, sometimes stop at New York, Baltimore, and Wilmington. Ships return from Gdynia by way of Bremerhaven to New York City only. Of course, as is always the case, ports and departure dates may change. Gdynia Line, however, always knows its precise sailing date a month in advance. They, in fact, urge passengers to call both then and at least four days before sailing to confirm the departure date and port of embarkation.

Round-trip fares on Gdynia Line amount to twice the one-way fare and can be arranged in advance.

Ventilation funnels frame a winch. *K. Helmer-Petersen*

Gdynia Line—Northern Europe

Type of Trip	From	To
one way	Port Newark (New Jersey), New York via Baltimore, Wilmington, and some North Carolina ports— return only to New York City	Rotterdam/Antwerp Bremerhaven/Hamburg Gdynia

AHOY!

The free baggage limit is 25 cubic feet, excess at $3.00 per cubic foot.
Cars can be carried as freight. Inquire as to current rates. Pets are not permitted.
Children's fares: under 1 year—10%; 1 to 12 years—half fare; over 12—full fare.
Passengers over 65 must have a doctor's certificate of good health.

Fare	Duration of Trip	How Often Sails	Number of Passengers
Off* On*			
$390; 440	10 days	weekly	12
$390; 440	12 days	weekly	12
$400; 450	14 days	weekly	12

*Off season—
Oct. 1 to May 31;
On season—
June 1 to Sept. 30

Gdynia Line
One World Trade Center, Suite 3557
New York, New York 10048
(212) 938-1900

Johnson Line

Vancouver, Seattle, Portland, San Francisco, and Los Angeles to Göteborg, Le Havre, London, and other possible ports via the Panama Canal, returning to one of the above West Coast ports

By now this may sound like an old refrain: Book early! However, in the case of Johnson Line's Swedish flagships to and from Europe, failing to apply for passage even as far as a year in advance could mean missing this delightful freighter voyage. As we describe the accommodations—and how entranced Johnson Line regulars are with each crossing—you'll understand!

Here are the particulars. Two Swedish cargo liners, the MSS *Axel Johnson* and the MSS *Annie Johnson,* boast luxurious staterooms for six passengers, or to be more precise, one so-called Owner's Suite and two extremely spacious double cabins. (The ships have no singles.) The Owner's Suite, situated on the boat deck and thereby guaranteeing a fine view at all times, is comprised of a sitting room, a bedroom with twin beds, and a private bath. If you are traveling with someone, you can reserve the Owner's Suite at a 25 percent surcharge on the regular fare. Should a solitary traveler want the suite, two full fares must be paid plus the surcharge. Also, if an adult accompanied by a youngster under the age of twelve desires the Owner's Suite, what would normally be a half fare for the under twelve becomes a full fare. Basically, the same rule applies to single travelers. To obtain exclusive use of a double cabin, an additional 50 percent of the fare must be paid.

To say that Johnson Line fans are satisfied with the service is an understatement. They lionize the entire experience, stressing superior food, service, and accommodations. Johnson Line's Swedish officers apparently go out of their way to delight and surprise the passengers, joining in for jovial "happy hours" before dinner. On one crossing during the Swedish holiday called Midsummer's Day, the crew produced a madcap celebration, beginning with cocktails and moving on to a bountiful smorgasbord dinner, followed by maypole dancing around the lounge's standposts.

LOADING MAILS AT THE DOCKS IN LONDON. 1934

Freighter takes on the royal mail along London wharve. *H. S. Williamson*

Only a weight watcher we know expressed dismay at the irresistible Johnson Line cuisine, which, combined with the rollicking good humor shared by crew and passengers, made dining a nearly bacchanalian affair.

Johnson Line—Northern Europe

Type of Trip	From	To
round trip	Vancouver, Seattle, Portland, San Francisco, and Los Angeles— returning to any one of the above.	Liverpool Le Havre Antwerp Rotterdam London Göteborg

AHOY!

Free baggage is 440 pounds, excess at $.10 per pound.

Cars can be taken as freight at prevailing rates. Pets are not accepted.

Children's fares: under 2 years—free; 2 to 3—quarter fare; 3 to 12—half fare; 12 years and over—full fare.

Persons over 75 not accepted. Passengers over 65 must be able to furnish a doctor's certificate of good health.

Fare	Duration of Trip	How Often Sails	Number of Passengers
$2050	18–20 days	every 4 weeks	6

Johnson Line
General Steamship Corporation Ltd.
400 California Street
P.O. Box 3450
San Francisco, California 94119
(415) 392-4100 Cable: GENSTEAMCO

Egon Oldendorff

New York and other East Coast ports to Antwerp and Hamburg, one way; New Orleans to Antwerp and Hamburg, one way.

 In regard to thriftiness and reliability, the German line Egon Oldendorff rates high. The line's many ships sail under the flags of Liberia, Singapore, Panama, and Somalia, transporting coal, grain, and machinery between numerous American ports and western Europe. Nine to twelve passengers travel on each ship in outside cabins—bright and well designed—with cot-type beds and private baths. Recently Egon Oldendorff added three new air-conditioned

Egon Oldendorff—Northern Europe

Type of Trip	From	To
one way	New Orleans	Antwerp and Hamburg
one way	New York and other East Coast ports	Antwerp and Hamburg

AHOY!

Free baggage is 1 cubic meter; the line suggests passengers not exceed this limit.
Cars are not accepted. Dogs (but not cats or birds) can come along upon permission of the line and master (captain) of the vessel. Vaccination and health certificates are required. Dogs may not, however, stay with passengers in cabins.
Children's fares: up to 1 year—$125; 1 to 12—half fare.
Age limit: 70 years.

vessels to the line; however, the majority of its ships are not air-conditioned. A great many of the ships have swimming pools. As for other facilities on board, there is a large dining saloon where passengers are joined by the captain (master, as he is called on Egon Oldendorff) and the senior officers. (On the line's larger ships there's an additional smoking saloon.) Since accommodations obviously vary considerably from ship to ship—even the sort of food is individual—when you book passage, find out whether the ship you'll be traveling on is new or old.

Keep your plans flexible. Departure and arrival dates depend solely on when, how, and at which port cargo is loaded. Promising to meet your old college roommate at the Gare du Nord on April 1 because you assume your ship docks in Antwerp on March 29 isn't a good idea. Tight scheduling and freighter travel make unpropitious partners!

Despite all our caveats, the courteous agents we talked to at Egon Oldendorff make their ships sound extremely attractive. In the words of its founder: "The quiet atmosphere on board will give you the opportunity for real relaxation . . . all on board endeavor to make the voyage an enjoyable and pleasant experience for every passenger." Considering the bargain-basement rates, what more could any globe-trotter ask?

Fare	Duration of Trip	How Often Sails	Number of Passengers
$487 (double) $537 (single)	12–15 days	every 3 weeks	9 to 12
$450 (double) $500 (single)	12–15 days	every 3 weeks	9 to 12

Egon Oldendorff
Biehl and Company Inc.
416 Common Street
New Orleans, Louisiana 70130
(504) 581-7788

Schluessel-Reederei Line

Tampa to Rotterdam and/or Vlissingen

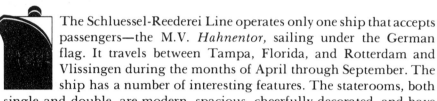

The Schluessel-Reederei Line operates only one ship that accepts passengers—the M.V. *Hahnentor*, sailing under the German flag. It travels between Tampa, Florida, and Rotterdam and Vlissingen during the months of April through September. The ship has a number of interesting features. The staterooms, both single and double, are modern, spacious, cheerfully decorated, and have private baths. But if you aim for more opulence, consider reserving the Owner's Suite, a tasteful combination of sitting room with desk, couch, cocktail table, and wall-to-wall carpeting, bedroom with double beds, comfortable chairs, dressing table, dresser, and large closet, as well as a big private bath. The surcharge for the Owner's Suite is $120. There's a catch, though: this stateroom is maintained by Schluessel-Reederei so that the line's executives can travel from Europe to the United States if they wish. Thus, no matter how far in advance you book the Owner's Suite, you're apt to be bumped to a double cabin on the rather unlikely chance that an official of Schluessel-Reederei suddenly decides to make the trip. (In that case, of course, your surcharge would be refunded.)

Other features of the ship include several public rooms for card games, music, and even dancing; a dining room, with a wizard of a chef specializing in both German and continental cuisine; a smoking room; and a lounge with verandah overlooking the swimming pool. There are laundry facilities on board, as well as a ship's store selling duty-free liquor, cigarettes, and other sundries.

Well-known sculptor Willard Boepple counts among his fondest childhood memories a westbound journey he made with his father on this line after a particularly wearisome summer of touring Italy, France, and Scandinavia. The graceful flow of days as they crossed became even more enjoyable when Willard, then a boy of thirteen, discovered the ship's cargo of tulips. "The holds were open," he relates, "so we could see them bobbing around—dozens and dozens of flats of tulips! I know tulips don't really have much of a scent, but those did smell . . . well, fresh and earthy."

For the most part, passengers on the M.V. *Hahnentor's* Atlantic voyage book one-way tickets. Upon arrival in Holland, the ship discharges its cargo and departs within no more than thirty-six hours. Schluessel-Reederei foresees no problem booking returns as long as you give adequate notice—say, several weeks. Another popular option with European-bound passengers is booking one way and flying the other. If this interests you, ask Schluessel-Reederei about a possible package deal.

Schluessel-Reederei K.G.—Northern Europe

Type of Trip	From	To
cruise	Tampa	Rotterdam and/or Vlissingen
one way	Tampa	Rotterdam and/or Vlissingen

AHOY!

Free baggage limit is 330 pounds per person. Check with Schluessel-Reederei for excess baggage rate.

Cars and other cargo are allowed. Check with the line for rates. Pets are not allowed.

Children's fares: under age 12—half fare.

Age limit: persons over 65 and children under 5 are not accepted.

Passengers accepted only during the months of April through September

Fare	Duration of Trip	How Often Sails	Number of Passengers
$1500	28 days	every 2 weeks	12
$750	14 days	every 2 weeks	12

Sea and Land Shipping Inc.
601 Twiggs St., Suite 400
Tampa, Florida
(813) 229-7284
Telex: WU 52-788
Cable: NYKEYSHIPS

Schluessel-Reederei K.G.
G.M.B.H.
P.O. Box 18—47 Am Wall 58-60
2800 Bremen, West Germany

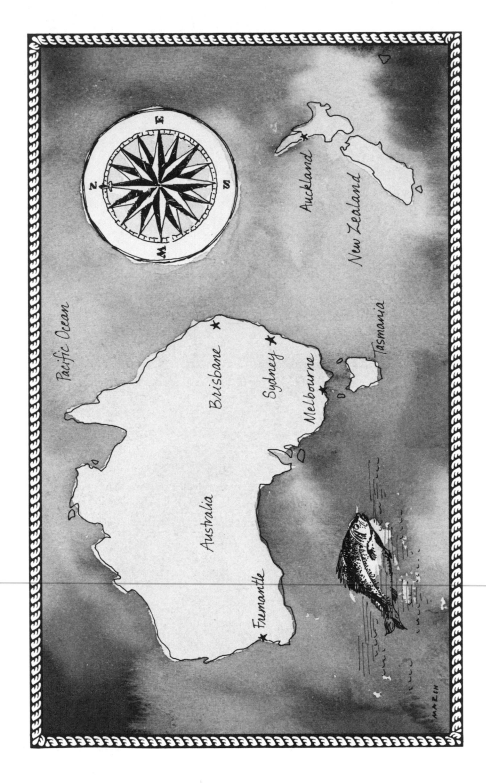

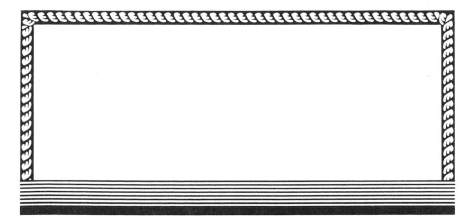

NINE

AUSTRALIA
AND
NEW ZEALAND

Farrell Line

**New York to Australia and New Zealand via the Panama Canal;
one-way trips from Brisbane and Auckland to New Orleans**

Beyond the fact that Farrell Line is a popular company among freighter buffs—if you have yet to read about the Farrell cruise in chapter 7, we'll review the basics at the end of this entry— several special features make the Australia–New Zealand junket especially hard to resist.

First, the route. Farrell Line container ships sail from New York through the Panama Canal—always a delight—to Brisbane, Melbourne, and then possibly a few other ports in Australia before finally arriving in New Zealand. Since boats sail every two weeks, round-trip passengers can leave the cruise, travel around Australia, and rejoin the cruise in either its last Australian port of New Zealand, providing, of course, prior arrangements are made with Farrell. A few stipulations: Farrell Line ships continue on to New Zealand; however, sometimes all passengers must disembark at the first Australian port of call. Those returning to the United States must embark at the last Australian port of call, usually Melbourne, or in New Zealand, and must disembark at the first U.S. port of call, usually New Orleans.

Second, the ships. The four C-6-type vessels that make this trip— SS *Austral Envoy*, SS *Austral Endurance*, SS *Austral Ensign*, and SS *Austral Entente*—are the newest in Farrell's fleet. All staterooms face forward and are situated high enough in the deckhouse to afford a spectacular view through your room's large picture window. Cabins, whether double or single, have connecting doors that can be converted to a suite for family or group travel. Each ship has a lounge, library, card rooms, and a huge dining room.

Earl Hatton, an inveterate globe-trotter, once worked
as a crew member on a Farrell ship, then took this same

Sydney harbor as viewed from the air, 1972   *Australian Tourist Commission*

Farrell Line—Australia, New Zealand

Type of Trip	From	To
cruise	New York	Brisbane Sydney Melbourne Auckland
one way	New York	Brisbane
one way	Brisbane or Auckland	New Orleans

AHOY!

The free baggage limit is 300 pounds. Ask Farrell for excess baggage rate.
Cars can be taken; pets are not allowed.
Children's fares: under 12 years—half fare.
Age limit: 75 years. Those over 65 must provide a Farrell Line medical certificate
signed by both passenger and doctor. Also, no children under 18 months of age.

Fare	Duration of Trip	How Often Sails	Number of Passengers
$2800; 3000	55 days	twice monthly	12
$1400; 1500	22 days	twice monthly	12
$1400; 1500	25 days	twice monthly	12

Farrell Line
1 Whitehall St.
New York, New York 10004
(212) 440-4200
Cable: FARSHIP

Ayers Rock in the Australian Outback

trip as a passenger. "Both years ago when I crewed and recently, the people going to Australia were like pioneers. Even if they aren't actually going off to the wilds of the outback to herd sheep, they have that spirit! I think the legend of Australia in the years when anyone could get a patent for a farm machine and homestead endures! I met the most interesting, original people on Farrell's Australian trip."

Earl also fondly recalls stopping in Panama, traditionally a time for hijinks in the rollicking nightclubs and sleazy bars of Panama City. "This time the passengers followed suit! A tribe of us made the rounds." Earl explained that the passage through the canal marks the beginning of the longest leg of the journey, and once the ship sails through, a decidedly more serene mood settles over the entire ship—crew, officers, and passengers—as they prepare for a pleasant Pacific crossing complete with balmy breezes and starlit nights.

He recalls how the ship was secured for sea after Panama. "The booms, used for loading and unloading cargo, are lashed to the deck—the hatches covered and metal beams mounted on deck. There was something final and consoling about that . . . as if we couldn't turn back."

A quick review: Farrell ships each have six staterooms that are larger than average, air-conditioned, situated outside, and all with private shower and bathroom. There are lounges, ample deck space, and a fine dining room with delicious American and continental food.

The Sydney bridge by day in this 1932 photo. Ships of great size can pass beneath the span.
Illustrated London News

A view of the Sydney Opera House

Perth Harbor, Australia, in 1965   © *Realities*

Knutsen Line

San Francisco to Fremantle, Australia, via Hong Kong, Manila, Singapore, Kobe, and Yokohama

This same Knutsen trip was described in chapter 3, thus we'll provide a recap of accommodation details at the end of the entry.

After the Oriental ports of call, your Knutsen ship docks in Fremantle where, we understand, the line's representatives are extremely helpful in arranging tours, hotels, and the like. Most veterans of this particular trip stress the charm of Perth, near Fremantle, and the abundance of fascinating side trips such as Tasmania or even New Zealand. One couple took the trans-Australian railroad to Ayers Rock, the world-famous sandstone mountain in the outback. Melbourne, too, is a lovely city, as is Sydney, which is noted for Manly Beach. In Canberra, Australia's capital, the attractions range from visits to Victorian monu-

Lounge of the *M.S. Lloyd Bakke,* Knutsen Line   *Knutsen Line*

Knutsen Line—Australia

Type of Trip	From	To
one way	San Francisco	Fremantle, Western Australia, via Hong Kong Manila Singapore Kobe and Yokohama

AHOY!

Free baggage limit is 350 pounds, not counting hand baggage. Ask Knutsen for excess baggage rate.

Cars can be taken at prevailing tariff rates. Pets are not permitted.

Passengers must show proof of smallpox vaccination within three years. Three cholera shots are required as well.

Children's fares: up to 1 year—quarter fare; 1 to 12 years—half fare; 12 years and up—full fare.

ments to sightings of flocks of sheep at any of the numerous sheep ranches in the vicinity.

Perhaps the most compelling of Australia's landmarks, however, is the Great Barrier Reef. Those who have been there say it's quite easy to arrange a bus to Brisbane, then on to Mackay, the tropical portion of the country. From there you go by boat to the reef and/or visit nearby Hook Island and Brampton Island.

Australians invariably charm visitors with their hearty wit and friendly manner. Also a great convenience is the fact that they speak English. In all, Australia is a land of bountiful cultural and topographical attractions. Ironically enough, it doesn't get nearly the tourist trade it deserves, a shocking fact when you consider its wholly unique wildlife (flowers to kangaroos) and the incredible aboriginal peoples who still inhabit central Australia just as they have for decades.

As for Knutsen Line, the ships provide a large lounge, dining saloon, plentiful deck area, and a swimming pool. Each ship carries twelve passengers housed in four double and four single cabins, all with private baths. The quality and variety of the ship's food is reportedly satisfying. Knutsen Line prefers to book passage one way, which allows you time to tarry in Australia, if you wish. Should you want to return promptly, consult both Knutsen Line and one of the freighter travel agents we've recommended to help with the arrangements.

Fare	Duration of Trip	How Often Sails	Number of Passengers
$2250; 2300	32 days	every 3 weeks	12

Knutsen Line
c/o Columbus Line
1 World Trade Center
New York, New York
(212) 668-9440

Knutsen Line
Bakke Steamship Corp.
650 California St.
San Francisco, California
(415) 433-4200

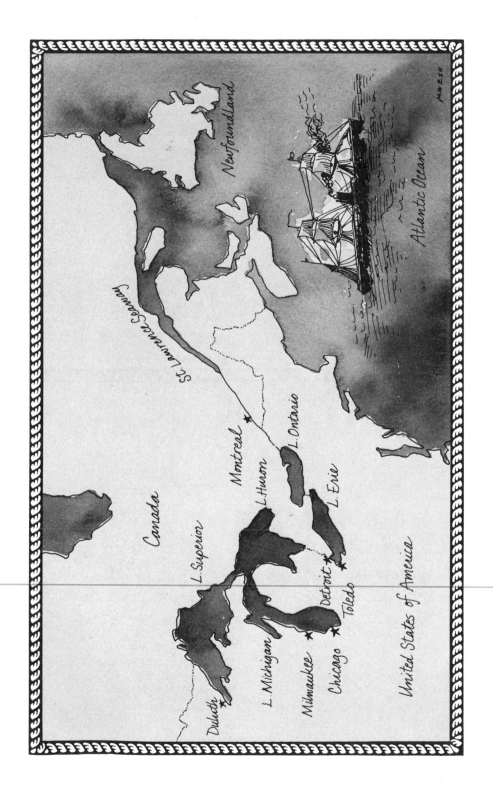

TEN

THE GREAT LAKES

Lykes Lines

Toledo, Duluth, Chicago, Milwaukee, or Detroit to Casablanca, Tangiers, Leghorn, Genoa, or Alexandria

If you've read about Lykes Lines trips to either the Orient or South America, you're familiar with the company. If not, we've included a summary of vital information at the end of this entry.

As a special convenience to midwesterners, we've included the freighter trips which depart from ports on or near the Great Lakes. Lykes Lines serves five such cities—Toledo, Duluth, Chicago, Milwaukee, and Detroit—though rarely does a ship bound for the Mediterranean call at all five. If you want to book this voyage, make sure your travel agent checks with Lykes to make sure you can depart from the port of your choice.

By the way, the same goes for ports at the other end. Sometimes a Mediterranean trip makes the rounds of all possible ports. More often, however, it selects them according to cargo demands.

On Lykes Lines, Great Lakes trips are seasonal. Only during the months of April through October and November, weather permitting, can ships safely make the transit up the St. Lawrence seaway.

Passengers who board in Duluth traverse Lake Superior, then, if the Lykes ship makes a stop at Milwaukee and/or Chicago, it enters Lake Michigan, travels south, then puts in at Milwaukee or Chicago before continuing north again. The last Great Lakes stops would be Detroit and Toledo on Lake Erie. Onward it steams into Lake Ontario and up the St. Lawrence seaway before entering the North Atlantic.

Veterans of this trip remark on a fascinating American adventure, touring the lakes, not to mention passage through the Welland Canal at the mouth of Lake Erie, which consists of eight locks spread over a twenty-eight mile distance. Under the best conditions (with few boats waiting), you can make it through the canal in about fifteen hours. As you may know, this canal and its locks are necessary because 325 feet separate Lake Erie from Lake Ontario. Each lock means either a forty-six foot drop or rise, depending on which way you're going. Once launched into the St. Lawrence seaway, your ship navigates seven more locks.

Now here's a quick briefing on Lykes Lines. The Lykes fleet includes five classes of freighters, including Pacer, Andes, Clipper, Pride, and "Roll-On, Roll-Off," although the majority of Great Lakes cruises utilize the Pacer, Andes, or "Roll-On, Roll-Off" type ships. All cabins are doubles, so if you're alone and don't wish to pay double, you may have to share a cabin. There are also a number of "preferred staterooms," distributed on a first-come, first-served basis, so make reservations for these cabins quickly. All cabins are situated outside and have private bathrooms.

Lykes Lines—The Great Lakes

Type of Trip	From	To
one way	Toledo	Casablanca
	Duluth	Tangiers
	Chicago	Leghorn
	Milwaukee	Genoa
	Detroit	Alexandria

AHOY!

Free baggage limit is 350 pounds. Ask Lykes Lines for excess baggage charge.
Pets, cars, and campers are not accepted.
Children's fares: 1 to 11 years—half fare; over 12—full fare.
Smallpox and cholera inoculations may be required. Ask Lykes Lines.

Fare	Duration of Trip	How Often Sails	Number of Passengers
$3200	60–70 days	once monthly (April through October or November)	12

Lykes Lines
300 Poydras Street
New Orleans, Louisiana 70130
(504) 523-6611

Lykes Lines
Melrose Building
Houston, Texas 77002

Lykes Lines
320 California Street
San Francisco, California 94104

Yugoslav Great Lakes Line

Montreal or Chicago to Rijeka, Naples, or various Spanish ports

From all reports, traveling aboard the MS *Split* from Montreal to Chicago for the Mediterranean and Yugoslavia is satisfying because it's a bargain and very interesting. Whether you embark from Chicago or Montreal, you still get a chance to pass through the scenic St. Lawrence seaway before entering the North Atlantic. From there it's a relatively short hop across.

Life aboard the MS *Split* is hardy, comfortable, and convivial. There are six double cabins, each with two baths and a shower (for some mysterious reason even the management can't explain). Accommodations include a spacious lounge and bar, which is always a popular gathering place, as well as the dining room. Food, described as "European," ranges from reliable stews and chops to tangy Mediterranean cheeses. And don't forget Yugoslavian wines, such as dry white Traminer, one of the world's best-kept oenophiliac secrets.

Most freighter buffs seem to make at least one trip on the MS *Split*, and reactions vary widely. Detractors mention that the crew often speak little English and that during winter crossings the heating systems don't quite do the trick. On the other hand, there are those who praise the zesty food while others complain about too much garlic and olive oil. We've heard, too, that officers and crew eat in a separate dining room on the MS *Split*. Again, some passengers welcome this privacy while others miss mingling with the crew. Everyone agrees on one thing, however. Staterooms are ideally situated with four big windows, an important asset as the scenery along the Great Lakes seaway and the Welland Canal is superb.

As you know, part of the fun of traveling by freighter is port-hopping. You'll notice from the chart that Yugoslav Great Lakes Line prefers not to specify its Spanish ports. But here's a hint: you can find yourself in Barcelona, Alicante, Bilbao, or who knows where. One lucky voyager ended up in Lisbon for three days before continuing on to Italy and Yugoslavia.

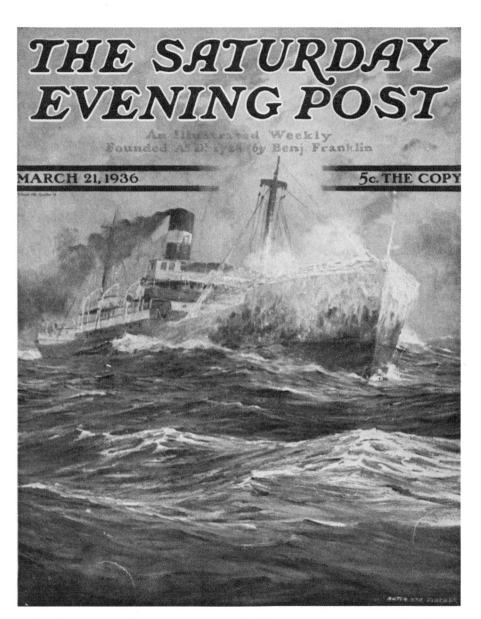

Modern freighter travel isn't quite the same as in 1936, when this *Saturday Evening Post* cover was published. *The Saturday Evening Post* © *1939, Curtis Publishing Co.*

Yugoslav Great Lakes Line—Mediterranean

Type of Trip	From	To
one way	Montreal	Rijeka (other ports of call: Naples, Leghorn, several
	Chicago	Spanish ports)
one way	Montreal	Naples
	Chicago	Naples
one way	Montreal	Leghorn
	Chicago	Leghorn
one way	Montreal	Spanish ports
	Chicago	Spanish ports

AHOY!

Free baggage limit is 270 pounds. Excess is $1.00 per twenty pounds.
Cars are accepted.
Pets may or may not be allowed, depending on the discretion of the ship's master.
Children's fares: under 12—half-fare.
Inoculations may be required. Check with consulates of countries.
Age limit: None on Yugoslav Great Lakes Line. All passengers over 65 must have
  medical certificate signed by a doctor and the ship's master.

Fare	Duration of Trip	How Often Sails	Number of Passengers
$690	21–28 days	every 2½ months	12
$750	21–28 days	every 2½ months	12
$610 $670	21–28 days	every 2½ months	12
$565 $600	21–28 days	every 2½ months	12
$540 $600	21–28 days	every 2½ months	12

Yugoslav Great Lakes Line
c/o Robert Reford
St. Sacrament Street
Montreal, Canada
(514) 849-5221

Polish Ocean Line

Chicago, Cleveland, and/or Montreal to Gdynia via Hamburg and Rotterdam

 By now it's apparent that freighter cruises originating in the Great Lakes area come with an automatic bonus—passage through the beautiful St. Lawrence seaway and a tour of the Great Lakes. But let's not forget Montreal. We've heard that Polish Ocean Line quite often tarries several days in this large, cosmopolitan Canadian city, where you can take a horse-drawn buggy down cobblestone streets to the old town, sight of Montreal's superb French restaurants. Or for contrast, hike over to Man and His World, the original

Polish Ocean Line—Great Lakes

Type of Trip	From	To
one way	Chicago and/or Cleveland	Gdynia via Hamburg and Rotterdam
one way	Montreal	Gdynia via Hamburg and Rotterdam

AHOY!

Free baggage limit is 275 pounds. Excess baggage is $.30 per pound.
Cars can be taken if space permits. Pets not allowed. No children allowed.
Inoculation may be required. Check with consulates of countries.
No age limit on Polish Ocean Line. All passengers over 65 must have medical certificate signed by a doctor and the ship's master.

location of Expo '67; it is located on two islands in the St. Lawrence River and is bursting with space-age architecture like the futuristic apartment complex called Habitat and continuing technological exhibits. Incidentally, Montreal's silent, rubber-wheeled subway, called the Metro, makes inner-city transportation easy as well as pleasant.

As for Polish Ocean Line, we describe it as a dependable, rugged travel bargain. Put it this way, when the line's major North American agent warns that the ship's staterooms aren't luxurious, you can have no illusions. Many have traveled happily on Polish Ocean Line ships, however, so don't be deterred. Double and single staterooms can be had with private baths. Each ship also has a lounge, bar, dining room, and the all-important snack bar. Food, called "International" by the line, tends toward rather starchy repasts, so bring your own brandied pears and caviar if you're unwilling to rough it, gastronomically speaking.

Veterans of this cruise unanimously praise the crew, who apparently take great pride in their ships and make great hosts, even when their command of the language limits conversation.

Fare	Duration of Trip	How Often Sails	Number of Passengers
$950	21 days	once monthly	12
$400	19 days	once monthly	12

McLean-Kennedy
410 St. Nicholas Street
Montreal, Canada
(514) 849-6111

President Fillmore of the American President Lines   *American President Lines*

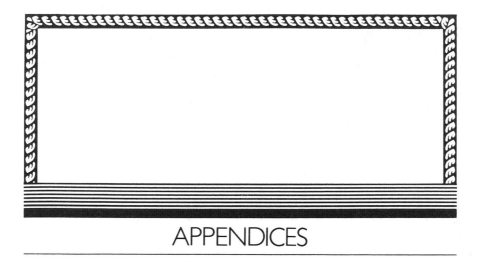

APPENDICES

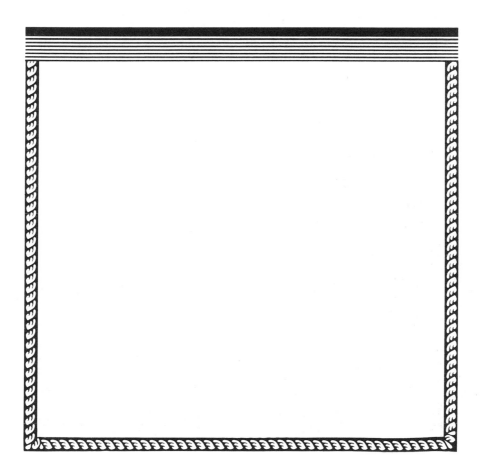

Foreign Port to Port

Here is a list of trips from one foreign port to another in whatever detail was feasible. Since information is sometimes hard to come by or frequently changes, your best bet is either to ply one of the better freighter agents for information or wait until you are aboard to contact the freighter companies directly.

Argentine Lines, Avenida Corrientes 389, Buenos Aires, Argentina (also: Linease Maritimas Argentinas, Cap House 9/12 Long Lane, London EC1A 9EP, England). Once every two months, ships leave Buenos Aires bound for two routes: (1) Liverpool, Le Havre, Antwerp, Rotterdam, Hamburg; (2) Genoa, Barcelona, Marseilles, Naples, Leghorn, Venice, Trieste.

Armement Deppe A.S. (Belgian), Kendall Globe Ltd., 52 London Wall, London EC2M 5TN, England. Frequent trips from Antwerp and Le Havre to San Juan and Veracruz.

Bank Line Ltd., 21 Bury St., London EC3A 5AU, England. One-way trips or cruises from Rotterdam to the South Pacific via Panama Canal (Papeete, Nouméa, Port Moresby, Lae, Rabaul, Honiara).

Belgian Line, Compagnie Maritime Belge, St. Katelinjnevest 61, B2000, Antwerp, Belgium (or Belgian Line Inc., 5 World Trade Center, New York, N.Y. 10048, 212-432-9050). Monthly trips from Antwerp, Rotterdam, Bremen, and Hamburg to Tenerife, Recife, Bahia, Rio de Janeiro, Santos, Rio Grande, Pôrto Alegre, Buenos Aires, Vitoria, Ilhéus, Bahia.

Bergen Line, 505 Fifth Ave., New York, N.Y. 10017, (212) 986-2711. Daily trips from Bergen, Norway, to Kirkenes, Norway, calling at up to thirty ports in Scandinavia.

Delta Line, 1 World Trade Center, New York, N.Y. 10048, (212) 432-4700. One-way trips every nineteen days from Rio de Janeiro to Callao.

Geest Line, Box 2, Barry, Glamorgan, South Wales, Barry (0446) 732333, Telex: 49428. One-way trips or cruises from Glamorgan, South Wales, to the Caribbean (Barbados, Grenada, Kingstown, Saint Lucia, and Dominica).

Hansa Line, 17 Battery Place, 5th Floor, New York, N.Y. 10004, (212) 425-6100. Departing Hamburg, Bremen, Rotterdam, or Antwerp for the Orient via two itineraries: (1) directly to Colombo to Sri Lanka and Bombay; (2) Port Said, Suez, Karachi, Bombay, Cochin, Madras, Rangoon, Chittagong, Colombo, and Calcutta.

JMM-Atlantic Line Ltd., 6-12 Newport Blvd., Newport West, Kingston, 15, Jamaica (or Furness Travel Ltd., 105 Fenchurch Street, London, EC3M 5HH, England). Monthly trip from Sheerness, Kent, to Montego Bay, Jamaica.

Losinjska Plovidba, P.O. Box 135, 51001, Rijeka, Yugoslavia. A variety of trips from Rijeka to: (1) Valletta, Benghazi, Tripoli, Tunis; (2) Trieste, Venice, Piraeus, Salonika, Istanbul, Izmir; (3) Salonika, Istanbul, Izmir; (4) Dakar, Monrovia, Abidjan, Tema, Luanda, Matadi, Douala, and several Mediterranean or Adriatic ports.

Polish Ocean Line, McLean Kennedy Inc., 410 St. Nicholas St., Montreal, Quebec, H2Y 2P5, Canada. Monthly South American trips from various North European ports bound for: (1) Lisbon, La Guaira, Buenaventura, Guayaquil, Callao; (2) Rio de Janeiro, Santos, Montevideo, Buenos Aires. Monthly trips from various northern European ports to Singapore, Bangkok, Hong Kong, and Yokohama. Monthly trip from northern European ports to Dar es Salaam, Mombasa, Aden, Port Sudan, and Las Palmas.

United Baltic Corp. Ltd., 24-26 Baltic St., London BC1Y 0TB, GB. Tel: 01-253-3456, Telex, 269783, Telegram, Orientteako. Frequent sailings from Hull and London to Turku, Helsinki, or Gdynia.

Freighter Travel Agents

Betty Tours and Travel Service
121–123 Chatham Road, 10th Floor, Flat C
Kowloon, Hong Kong
Cable: BETOURS, Telephone: K-681251 or K-674627

Freighter Cruiser Service
5925 Monkland Avenue, Suite 103
Montreal, Quebec H4A 1G7
Telephone: (514) 481-0447

President Van Buren of the American President Lines   *American President Lines*

A Lykes liner *Lykes Lines*

Freighter World Cruises Inc.
180 S. Lake #335F
Pasadena, California 91101
Telephone: (213) 449-3106

Maggi Horn
601 California Street
San Francisco, California 94108
Telephone: (415) 421-9800

McLean-Kennedy
410 St. Nicholas Street
Montreal, Canada
Telephone: (514) 849-6111

Pearl's Freighter Tips
175 Great Neck Road, Suite 306F
Great Neck, New York 11021
Telephone: (212) 895-7646 or (516) 487-8351

Robert Reford
St. Sacrament Street
Montreal, Canada
Telephone: (514) 849-5221

Taylor Travel Service Inc.
3959 Main Street
Buffalo, New York 14226
Telephone: (716) 837-7588